Grave Misgivings

Grave Misgivings

Mason Stone

Red Pine Publishing

CONTENTS

Preface

This is dedicated to my LittleOne.

This book is a work of fiction. It is set in a fictional town in New England. Certain historical or geographic references may be made to enhance the setting, time and place.

All persons, organizations, and circumstances are fictional and any resemblance to any person living or dead is purely coincidental.

ISBN: 978-1-989386-13-2

1

This is the quiet little town of Earlsdale, New Hampshire. Population: 11,411.

Actually—11,410, since one resident has just been murdered.

New Hampshire is—and always has been—a notable part of New England.

An integral part of the United States of America since the Revolutionary Days of the 1780s.

It was the first of the Thirteen Colonies to become independent in 1776 and establish its own State Constitution. By 1788, its people had ratified the Declaration of Independence and embraced the Constitution of the proud new nation.

Its people have always been fiercely independent and have made their State motto one which reflects that spirit: *Live Free or Die*.

Today it is America's fifth smallest state with only a million and a half inhabitants.

It has no income tax and limited sales tax. In 2013 it had the lowest poverty rate in the United States. The median income is over $73,000 yearly.

At least one-tenth of its industry is related to the leisure and hospitality industry. The wild natural beauty of mountains and seashore make New Hampshire a very popular destination—both for travel and for settlement.

Trace Edger is a settler. He is originally from Washington State with a law enforcement background.

In Earlsdale—he is a popular attorney—with always a kind word or greeting for the townspeople. He is always busy at his downtown Main Street office, but he makes time for what is important in the community.

In fact, what happens in the community is a bit of a personal mission of his.

Since the local police force of four is often outnumbered, overworked, and underpaid, Trace Edger puts in lots of hours of his own time investigating issues that come up in Earlsdale.

By *issues*—we are talking about crime. As a former police lieutenant in a detective bureau, he brings experience and has—how shall we say it?—a nose for trouble.

He is not alone in that regard, either.

Geraldine Moore is a local reporter who might well be called Trace Edger's 'sidekick' since the two of them are often seated at the beloved local diner discussing and speculating over steaming cups of Danni's good coffee.

The town has a city hall with a feisty lady mayor, two banks, a post office, a Chamber of Commerce, a community center and a library, a small medical center—in fact, all the amenities you would hope to find in a town of this size.

They have a newly-renovated water supply and sewage system, hi-speed Internet, a cinema and scads of new condominiums going up in vacant lots and grassy fields. Earlsdale is on a growth spurt.

One of the other charming features of small towns is that everybody knows everybody else's business.

Regardless of socioeconomic status and income, everyone gets their hair cut, everyone shops for groceries, their children and grandchildren go to school; there are invisible but significant lines of connection and communication that bind this community in a way that both protects and exposes one another.

That's just how things are. Nobody complains. Earlsdale is like a living organism which is always aware of itself but you would have to live here to really know that.

***

Pete McCoy has to know his town—he is the Chief of Police. He is the symbol of Justice and of the Rule of Law that is grounded in our Constitution—the very DNA of these United States.

He also drives a crappy old Dodge Charger, shaves every other day, rarely takes his gun out of his drawer at the police station, and is seemingly addicted to cappuccino.

He probably spends more time reading bulletins from State and Federal law enforcement than actually making his presence felt on the streets and byways of Earlsdale.

Other than parking tickets, he and his three trusty officers have little actual policing to do on a day-to-day basis.

Sometimes they make a little overtime patrolling a private function, or supervising a parade or festival with fireworks down at the bay, or organizing a funeral procession—like today.

One of the town's most highly regarded patriarchs—Magnus Magnussen—has suddenly and unexpectedly passed away. In a small pond, when large stones drop—they make ripples.

Known as a town benefactor and philanthropist, old Magnus was a staunch and regular at Mass at St. John's Cathedral at 4th and Tom St. in the downtown area. He was close to Father McIsaac—the resident priest and chaplain.

Father McIsaac is no spring chicken himself—having presided over the local flock for forty-one years this month.

So the turnout for Magnus' funeral was impressive and the church and all nearby parking was completely full. The part-time organist played *Sonata Pathetique* by Beethoven and many parishioners were seen to openly weep.

At the wishes of the family, this was a closed casket ceremony and flowers were laid in bunches only in specified areas. The service began and finished with prayers, with a brief word from Father McIsaac in between.

Sometimes at a church service the good Father would wander off into scriptural interpretations that were lengthy and obscure. Of course, everyone tolerated this; he was an ecclesiastical authority and spoke on behalf of the Church and of Our Lord.

His closing words today were no exception. *"And inasmuch as ye have done it to the least of these, so have ye done it unto Me. Amen."*

The children were naturally the first out the doors into the bright sunshine with glad shouts and shenanigans. Father McIsaac had a kind word with each congregant in their turn as they too left the shade and quiet of the magnificent structure.

The organ played and the light streamed in through the brilliant crimsons and royal blues of the stained-glass windows, giving the church a genuine feel of holiness and sanctity.

At least, that's what many people said—and it was to Father McIsaac's credit that the building fund account was always kept full by his regular call for donations.

Chief McCoy and his men lined out the procession heading to the cemetery on the far side of Highway 9 which forms the southern border of the town.

Lights flashing and moving at ten miles an hour, Chief McCoy took Lakeshore Drive to Waterwheel Drive whereon he turned left and led the string of cars south to the highway and then right to the entrance to the cemetery—which itself was across the road from Sayonara Funeral Services—where all the usual arrangements would have been made.

The plot had been prepared by the funeral home. Some children found it disturbing to see the lovely green sod peeled back and a yawning chasm carved into the moist brown earth ready to receive the mortal remains of a human being and clung to their mothers.

The local gravedigger boys Daniel and Darby O'Malley were lowering a shiny wooden box on strapping with sturdy arms—down into the darkness of its last resting place.

Parents shushed and held out their arms to keep curious little ones from peering and possibly toppling into the hole.

Father McIsaac always wrote his own material so the eulogy was eloquent and respectful.

At its conclusion, the O'Malley boys wasted no time shovelling the soil and stones into the grave—again drawing shrieks of excitement from the boys who were chasing madly around the tombstones.

The crowd had been invited by a local doyenne—of considerable wealth—to her mansion on the hill west of town. Monika von Travesty was the widow of a German automobile magnate who had retired in The Granite State and expected to live out his days fishing and hunting pheasants.

Regrettably, his days were numbered. In double digits. His last foray into the woods had apparently taxed his weak heart and he was carried home pale and lifeless.

The couple were childless and so Frau von Travesty lived in isolated splendor with a simply superb view of Lake Wendigo and its blue expanse. Her home could rightfully compare to a palace back in the Old Country and occupied at least two of the ten acres of property up off Skyline Drive.

The interior was nothing short of lavish—Austrian crystal chandeliers, hand-carved woodwork by craftsmen from Europe, marble floors, marble fixtures, five washrooms, floor-to-ceiling windows on the lake side, skylights in the bedrooms. The works.

Every detail whispered opulence to the point of grandiosity.

Its owner was outfitted in much the same fashion—with designer gowns, glittering necklaces and brooches—enough gold on her neck and wrists to make a pirate want to kidnap and ransom her off just for the jewelry.

"Daahling!" was how she greeted all her guests accompanied by a gesture of a kiss on one cheek that never made contact with anyone.

She had servants—who had hired caterers to serve afternoon tea for all of the mourners from the graveside service.

The food was lavish, too. Delicacies that actually gave rise to the German word 'delicatessen' and had an abundance of flaky pasties cooked with butter, farm-fresh berries, German sausage and bratwurst, cheese that had aged in European smokehouses, cheesecake that melted in your mouth.

This was more like a celebration than a funeral. Old Magnussen would have hated to have missed it!

***

Meanwhile, on the other side of town—in the venerable local diner called Danni's—Trace Edger, Attorney-at-Law and journalist or partner-in-crime as he called her—Geri Moore—were having a late breakfast.

"Got a call from Pete McCoy this morning," said Trace stirring his coffee.

"Oh? What about?" Geri was a reporter with a reputation for digging deeper. She was good—and since she had partnered up with one of the best lawyers in the state—she was even better!

"He got a call from a woman named Helen Thorne. Lives up on The Heights on Opal Crescent. Husband works in town in his own software firm. Didn't show up for dinner last night."

Trace lifted his head and arched an eyebrow at his companion.

"And....let me guess....isn't picking up on his cell," said Geri waving at Marla for more coffee.

"Missing persons reports have a nasty habit of morphing into nightmares," said Trace. "We know that better than anyone, don't we, Geri?"

"Yeah. And my woman's intuition is ringing a bell on this one! What does Pete want us to do?"

"Usual. Keep our eyes and ears open.

We might consider paying Helen Thorne a visit. Tell her the Chief of Police sent us.

Might help her feel supported by the law enforcement officials and at the same time—yield some information that might be useful down the road."

"Assuming there *is* a road, Trace.

Maybe he stayed over at someone's and his battery died, or maybe he had too much to drink and slept it off in one of those cheap motels out on Highway 9."

"And maybe aliens abducted him for his computer expertise and he's on the far side of the Moon in one of their bases," said Trace a tad sarcastically.

"Well, then, Counselor—your car or mine?"

***

"Helen Thorne? How do you do? I am Trace Edger, an attorney in town. Police Chief Pete McCoy asked us to drop by and see if you were okay and if you had heard from your husband...."

"*Miles*. His name is Miles. Please come in."

Helen Thorne was an attractive thirty-something housewife who kept a tidy but tastefully decorated home in an upscale part of Earlsdale.

Earlsdale had the normal socio-economic stratifications that any American town or city would have.

There were working class people—mainly singles or single-parents who lived more downtown, and there were uber-rich who lived like Monika von Travesty or the late Thetford Minah up on the ridge in relative splendor.

And there were lots more middle-class folks with decent jobs or healthy retirement packages who lived in 2700 square-foot, two-storey homes—that were either new construction or newly renovated—situated in nice neighborhoods on tree-lined streets.

Considering the median income in New Hampshire is close to $75,000 per capita per annum, this made perfect sense. This state had old money and new money—and just money in general.

The state had the eighth highest number of millionaires in the country. Not bad for the fifth smallest state in the Union.

"Can I offer you a cup of coffee or tea?" said Helen in that soothing suburban voice that people pick up as their finances and social standing improve.

"No, thanks. First off—let us assure you that our excellent investigative capabilities of local police are excellent. Chief McCoy will use all of the resources at his disposal to bring a successful conclusion to the matter of your husband's...ah...absence, shall we say."

Trace was an attorney—and attorneys have silver tongues—which can make the mundane sound magnificent. In any case, Trace was a genuinely caring guy and any of his clients will tell you that.

Geri found it hard not to giggle. Trace's description of the local police 'investigative capabilities' was stretching the truth just a bit.

Chief McCoy had three officers—and they worked hard, but honestly—Pete McCoy relied heavily on Trace and Geri to do any 'investigating'.

Which is precisely why they were sitting in the living room of Helen Thorne.

"Can you tell me what his daily routine looks like?" said Trace taking out a yellow legal pad and scribbling on it, trying to get his pen to write.

"Well, he leaves for work by 8:00am. He doesn't need to but it's a habit he got into when he had his company in Nashua. He's a computer engineer. Or software engineer. A geek he calls himself."

"Go on," said Trace.

"He goes out for sushi most days at lunch to the Japanese sushi takeout on Alfred and Commerce Drive. It's owned by Koreans although they call it 'authentic Japanese'."

"And after work? Does he normally work long hours?" asked Trace.

"If he does—he *always* calls. Occasionally he will have a project with a deadline and will stay late at the 'shop'—as he calls it. But most days he is home by 7:00pm—even if he swings by the grocery to pick something up."

Helen smoothed her skirt and carefully kept her knees parallel and close together. *Private school* thought Geri.

"But last night—or was it the night before?—he did not come home, is that correct?" Trace continued.

"It is so unlike him," said Helen with a wrinkle across an otherwise perfectly smooth forehead.

"Could he have stayed with a friend? Or family? And somehow forgot to call?" Geri was horning into the conversation now as the tension started to ratchet up.

"Miles has no relations here. They live in Virginia. My brother lives in Massachusetts outside of Boston. And apart from a few couples we play euchre with, no real friends he would visit."

"No children?" said Trace.

"We cannot have children, unfortunately," said Helen with a doleful look.

"Does your husband ever talk about...having...problems at work?" said Trace tactfully.

"Enemies," said Geri much less tactfully, as was her personality. Direct—if nothing else!

"Why, I don't think so," said Helen. "Why would he have any enemies? He is the sweetest guy and treats everyone with respect."

"We are just shooting in the dark here, Helen," said Geri. "Something has happened to your husband. I'm going to say that even though he's only been gone less than 48 hours.

I want you to call us at this number if he returns or if he calls or if someone calls to say they've seen him or been with him. Okay?"

"Alright," said Helen softly. The presence of persons who were investigators was starting to get it into her head that there might be some difficult times ahead.

Geri handed her a business card belonging to *Trace Edger, J.D. 221B Main St., Earlsdale, N.H. 03244*

Helen Thorne closed the door quietly. The sun was behind the tall red maples on Opal Crescent. Darkness would begin to fall in about six hours.

***

Five Days Earlier...

Sayonara Funeral Services on Hwy. 9 was the only funeral home in Earlsdale. So it got all the business.

Ken Covidson was the proprietor and had been for some years. Only one other mortician worked for him, although he also had an office administrator cum bookkeeper who had an office of her own.

"There's a nice letter from the Magnussens, Ken. A card, actually, a 'thank-you'card."

The secretary Sharon Smith was a down-to-earth, sensible wife and mother of two who lived in the new condos out on Pleasant Drive. Her husband worked for the City Works Department.

"Was there a check in it?" said Ken.

Bottom line for Ken was getting the payments. 'Funerals and embalming weren't cheap' he often said.

"Don't see it. Maybe I'll give them a call this week."

"Please do, Sharon. I've got bills to pay too! That family has enough money to buy a Caribbean island!"

Ken was cleaning up in the mortuary with rubber gloves and bleach. Bleach was cheap and worked as well as any of those fancy cleaning products that they flog to practitioners in the industry.

Sharon routed the call down to the embalming room in the morgue.

"Ken Covidson. How can I help you?"

The voice was female but not very easy to understand. Ken took off his gloves and sat on a stool.

"You do peekups?" The voice was mechanical like a bot and didn't talk like normal people do.

"If you mean: do we drive to you to recover a body for processing in our funeral home—the answer is 'yes'."

"I give you address for peekup." The voice gave a location out on Twilight Road just at the edge of town toward the eastern rim of the large broad valley in which the town was situated.

"When?" said Ken.

"Tonight." the voice said.

"I need the paperwork: death certificate, ID of deceased, cash only."

"It will be ready," said the voice in the same mechanical cadence. No questions about the cost or getting a receipt for payment. Nothing.

Ken cleaned up and got his mini-van ready for his eight-o'clock appointment. He decided to wear a shirt and tie because you always want to make a good impression.

No one saw him leave or return. Sharon was home fixing dinner for her family by 7:30pm.

The corpse was stiff with *rigor mortis* which made it easier to carry the body to the back of the van.

They had just sat the guy up in a lawnchair!

No lights were on, no one to say a last farewell. There was a ziploc bag in the dead man's lap.

Looking inside, Ken just scanned the required documents quickly and found a tidy ten grand in the envelope provided.

Large bills. That usually means 'no questions' and 'no paper trail'. Ken had seen it before.

Once inside the gate in the underground entrance, Ken brought a gurney to lay the deceased person on and wheeled him into the basement of the building.

For tonight, Ken's guest would sleep at a cozy 34 degrees Fahrenheit in the refrigeration cabinet that every morgue must have.

2

"Mr. Edger, please." The woman on the phone sounded very nervous to Penny—Trace's unflappable secretary and official muffin-maker.

"One moment, please." Trace took the call on his landline with his feet up. He never wore street shoes in his office for that reason. No footprints on his files!

"*Trace Edger.*" His voice was all business when he didn't know the caller.

"Mr. Edger? It's Helen Thorne. The missing-husband lady? You paid me a visit with your friend."

"*Oh, yes. How are you, Helen. Any word*?"

"I am very distressed, Mr. Edger. I have to see you. Shall I come to your office?"

"*Is that convenient? Do you mind if my partner is here? Good! How about three? Great. See you then.*"

Trace dialed Geri. "*You free? You might wanna get over here. Helen Thorne has a problem. See ya!*"

Penny showed Mrs. Thorne into the inner office where Trace spent 75% of his week.

"Sit down, Helen," he said. "You remember Geri Moore?"

Helen Thorne wasted no time getting to her point.

"I was in the liquor store. Getting wine. Right next to me was a man who was taking bottles down and then putting them up again—which became annoying."

"That's not against the law," said Trace. He twisted the cap off a small bottle of mineral water.

"But—Mr. Edger. I saw his arm! On his right wrist he wore a wristwatch. A Rolex Perpetual Oyster.

This one had certain features that very few Rolexes have. The same unique engraving marks that Miles' Rolex has. I know—I bought it for his 40th birthday and paid a pretty penny, too!"

Geri looked at Trace. Trace looked at Helen. "You're sure about this?" he said.

"Without a doubt. That man was wearing Miles' watch. Now where on *earth* did he get it, I'd like to know?"

"Any idea who the man was?" asked Geri.

"Haven't a clue. I was just about to summon the nerve to question him but he seemed to sense me staring at him and he bolted for the door."

"Too bad," said Trace. "We could see if the CCTV picked him up on camera."

"He drove off. In a white minivan. I got the plate on my iPhone here."

"Helen, you are marvelous!" said Trace, copying down the plate number. It was a New Hampshire plate.

"What should I do?" Helen Thorne asked. The thought that her husband's watch was no longer on her husband had galvanized her to action.

"I will have the police trace the plate and we will question the owner of the van. If this turns out to be a theft, you can rest assured that he will be charged and your husband's watch returned," said Trace.

Remember, he may have *found* it if for some reason Miles *lost* it," Geri hastened to add.

After Mrs. Thorne left, Geri asked the obvious.

"Lost it *how*, big boy? Went swimming at the club and left it in the shower?"

"That's what I intend to ask Mr. White Minivan," said Trace.

***

"*Let me read you that plate again.*" Trace was speaking with someone at the DMV. As a lawyer he knew little back doors into large bureaucracies.

"*Covidson. Kenneth C. 4409 Highway 9, Earlsdale. Okay, gotcha. Thanks!*"

Sharon Smith picked up the phone.

"Sayonara Funeral Services. This is Sharon. How may I help you today?"

She had the perfect phone voice and—after all—most people phoning were not in great emotional shape and needed a cheery welcome from someone working in what is traditionally called 'the dismal trade'.

"Mr. Covidson is not available at the moment. Can I have him return your call?"

Trace said 'no' and hung up.

He called Pete. "*You free for coffee? See you there.*"

As the weather forecast was good and tourist season was showing promise, the one and only Beanbags in town was full—packed!

But Pete always got special treatment and they served him ahead of the other customers. When Trace arrived at the table, Pete had their cappuccinos with napkin and stir-stick all laid out nicely.

"You should be a barista, Pete," said Trace cheerfully. "Nobody's gonna put a bullet in you and you don't need to carry all that hardware. Those cuffs must weigh a pound. Do you have to carry them everywhere?"

Pete knew Trace quite well and could take the ribbing in good humor.

"So what's on the menu, Counselor?" Pete said blowing on his coffee.

Trace outlined the situation with Helen Thorne and her alleged sighting of the Rolex.

"So this guy Covidson maybe has something to do with Thorne's disappearance? *Covidson*. Sounds like a disease."

"Very possible, Pete. I called his place of work and I'm thinking of cruising out there. Want to ride shotgun with me?"

"You think I have nothing to do as Chief of Police but sit around all day drinking coffee and chatting?"

Pete and Trace could keep this up all day. But Trace was onto something that Pete needed to keep an eye on. Missing person's case. Never good.

"Can I finish my drink or you think we have to catch this guy before lunchtime?"

Pete slurped the bottom inch of foam from his cup and put on his hat. Pete had never been seen out of uniform in the three years Trace Edger had been practicing law in Earlsdale.

***

Pete showed his badge to Sharon Smith who bade them sit while she fetched her boss.

"These places creep me out," said Pete in a hushed voice. "You know there's dead people just lying everywhere in these pink satin caskets. When I die..." but he was cut off by the arrival of Ken Covidson—the owner and licensed mortician and funeral director.

"Why don't we go into my office?" he suggested. "Hold my calls, Sharon, please."

"Do you own a white GMC van bearing plate WXYZ-401?" Pete read from his notebook.

"Why *yes*. Is there a problem, Officer?"

"Would you mind exposing your right wrist, Mr. Covidson?" Pete was on him.

"What is this about, exactly?" Covidson squeaked. He tugged on his jacket to reveal a gleaming wristwatch that seemed too big for his scrawny arm.

"We have reason to believe, Mr. Covidson, that this watch was stolen from its rightful owner. We want to know how it came into your possession."

"Stolen? You think I stole it?" His voice was going off the register at the high end.

"Got another explanation?" said Pete adjusting himself in his seat—body language that Trace could read that said Pete was enjoying himself.

"Okay, I will tell you the honest-to-gawd truth, Officer. This watch came off a body I retrieved last Friday evening. The individual in question was not slated for embalming and there was no one asking for a service at the cemetery.

So I prepared the body and removed all jewellery before I placed him into a coffin."

"And where's that coffin now?" said Pete.

"In the ground," said Covidson. "In a burial plot across the street. In the cemetery."

Trace took out a stick of gum and offered one to Pete; he took it.

"So can you show me the death certificate and ID that goes along with that?" said Pete.

Covidson grew pale and turned behind to his filing cabinet and shuffled some paper.

At length, he placed the documents on his desk and Pete snatched them up.

"*Miles Thorne*? That's what this driver's license says. And insurance card." Pete handed the death certificate to Trace.

"This...ah...looks suspicious," Trace began. "Cause of death is listed as MI—heart attack. The signature on this is unreadable but it doesn't look like George Roy's scrawl. I know his scrawl—and this isn't it!"

Trace sat up and was alternating his attention between Pete and Covidson.

"Miles Thorne was only 42 years old; a bit young for a cardiac event," Trace went on. "Tell me about the place you 'retrieved' the body. Who was handing him off to you?"

"Well, that's the thing. Nobody. I mean, there was nobody. Just the deceased...ah...left in an obvious place for me to pick up.

That was the arrangement I made over the phone," he said meekly.

"You got a phone number?" said Pete.

"Sorry. It showed only *Private Caller* on the screen."

"How convenient," said Pete ironically. "So we pick up a dead guy, prep him for burial, remove his expensive timepiece cause it would be a shame to see *that* go into the grave with him, and everything is hunky-dory."

"I swear, Officer. That's what happened. The law says unclaimed items from deceased clients remain the property of the funeral home."

"Except for two little things," Trace chimed in. "One: the wife of the deceased wants the watch back, and two, she is going to want to know how her husband ended up dead and buried without her knowledge or consent."

“Three!” said Pete. “The local police are gonna want to know how he ended up deceased and who helped him get there!”

3

"Well he was lucky; she could have pressed charges," said Pete.

"Speaking as a lawyer, I doubt the charge of theft would stick. Reason being is that theft, robbery and assault only apply to victims who are *alive,*" Trace was saying.

"In civil law, we have something called Detinue & Conversion—meaning you kept something of value and tried to sell it or cash in on it. But if the plaintiff is *deceased*, the courts have no one to award judgement to.

Let's face it, Pete—dead people have very few rights. Maybe someone should start a movement."

"Isn't that what zombies are?" said Pete picking up the phone.

"That was the lawyer for the Magnussen Family.

He got Ken Covidson to admit that he does not actually know—is not actually *sure*—who was in the coffin that was lowered into old Magnussen's grave.

They want it dug up. They have filed for an exhumation order. This could get interesting," Pete said.

"So then what Covidson told us—that he is not clear *who* went in *which* grave that Saturday—has some validity to it," said Trace.

"Remind me before I die to make funeral arrangements in another city," said Pete drily.

***

Geri, Trace and Pete were enjoying Danni's All Day Breakfast with unlimited coffee refills. It came with eggs any style, bacon any style, toast and hash browns (or homefries Greek style if Demetrios was cooking).

This is where they got most of their work done. The diner had old-fashioned high back booths with leather comfort and lots of privacy if you were having that kind of conversation.

Geri started. "We are—gentlemen—in the same boat we always find ourselves. One corpse—two options. Either it was homicide or it wasn't.

If it *was*, then we have several possibilities available for our consideration." Geri took a long swallow of coffee and waved at Marla for a refill.

She continued. "The first person of interest in any homicide that has domestic written all over it is the *spouse*. Most domestic assaults are perpetrated by a spouse—usually male.

In our case, we have a weird-looking mortician who buries people without checking who they are—only that the color of their money is good.

And helps himself to any goodies that may have been overlooked by the relatives—such as cash, jewellery and who-knows-what else!"

"I like the way your mind works," said Pete appreciatively. He was poking the burnt rind off a strip of bacon which itself was burnt beyond all recognition as food.

He chewed thoughtfully. Then he said: "I like your first idea; but we have to go through the usual steps of analysis to see what advantage Helen Thorne would gain by having her darling dispatched!"

"You mean Motive, Means & Opportunity?" said Geri.

"Mm-hmm," said Pete crunching the next strip of blackened bacon in his mouth. His face was the picture of happiness. It was amazing to Geri that the Chief of Police could be appeased by such a simple thing.

"Let's start with Motive, then," Geri said. "Why do wives kill their husbands?"

"Insurance," Pete said immediately. "That's an easy one. Trace?"

"Jealousy. He was involved with someone else and Helen found out."

"But..." Geri said triumphantly, "...the only one with all *three* factors is the *mortician*. He was no doubt paid by some unknown person or persons, he has the full range of poisons in his mortuary, and spends most of his working time getting them ready for their eternal rest."

"Plus, he's the one that puts them in the ground so the evidence is hidden more or less permanently," said Pete. Pete was starting on his toast. Trace noticed he was also peeling off the crust as he did with bacon. This was becoming a thing.

"When is the exhumation scheduled?" Geri asked.

"Soon as this rain stops, I guess," said Pete. "This is—what? Wednesday? Then Saturday if we're lucky."

***

The O'Malley boys were all ready with the shovels. They only use the backhoe for the initial dig; then they are as careful as archaeologists when they disturb a grave.

Daniel said there's an old Irish superstition that to disturb a grave is to awaken a ghost, so both boys were wearing dangling crucifixes prominently around their necks.

The Magnussen Family sent two representatives to attend: the widow Annike and her son, Olaf.

Also present was Geri Moore, reporter for the *Hillsboro Examiner,* Trace Edger—a local attorney, and Pete McCoy and Danno McFee from the Earlsdale Police Station on First Avenue.

The command to dig was given by the only other person present: Ken Covidson, the Sayonara Funeral Services director and final authority on *who* goes *where* in Earlsdale Cemetery!

The O'Malleys were not just gravediggers and maintenance men. They were also farmers with a few acres of their own northeast of town in a particularly fertile band of soil. They had tried chickens and cows but gave up and now farmed local apples—which were much easier, and did not require fencing.

At length, a metal spade clanged on the box and they slid into the hole and began strapping it for the lifting phase.

Most fancy caskets are for viewing; the body itself goes into a cheap wood or cardboard coffin in the casket—and that coffin is what generally goes in the ground at burial. Unless the client pays more.

The General Price List (GPL) is the standard for rates and prices in the funeral industry.

Every thing is available from flowers to expensive, stainless or bronze sealed caskets—but they run as much as $10,000 so cannot fit the budget of everyone.

Sayonara gave people the option to rent. Of course, they could opt to purchase and to have the whole business put in the grave; as Ken Covidson liked to say: "It's *their* money!"

Most funerals in the United States run about $10,000 or so—without the casket—which would make it quite costly.

Covidson knew that people would spend as much as they could afford to in order to see their loved ones laid to rest appropriately. Sayonara was a full-service facility for that reason.

Straining hard, the boys cleared the sides with the pine box and set it on the turf a few feet back from the edge.

Now it was Ken Covidson's turn—since he alone had the legal authority to do what he was about to do.

With a mallet and chisel, he whacked at one edge of the lid and pried. He did this right around the whole coffin. Then—with one final squeal of the crowbar—the lid slid up to rest on the nails and the O'Malleys gingerly lifted it off and put it aside.

Everyone peered into the shallow coffin. It was not an everyday thing and most people would find it utterly distasteful to stare down at a decomposing corpse.

A gasp went up from the small knot of onlookers. Annike Magnussen crossed herself, then collapsed on the sod.

Pete and Geri gawked at what they saw. Trace Edger surreptitiously aimed his iPhone in a downward direction.

Ken Covidson himself was apparently surprised as well. He had instructed the O'Malley boys to fill the various graves with the coffins or caskets sitting on the loading dock at the funeral home.

He had seemingly overlooked labeling them so each would go to its proper assigned plot.

Pete looked at the photograph he had been given. Then he looked at Trace.

Pete decided this was *his* duty so he announced in his best public voice: "Ladies and gentlemen, *Miles Thorne.*"

Pete had a word with McFee—who then told Covidson that the body would need to be confiscated for the purpose of having an autopsy done.

Covidson and McFee were still arguing when Mrs. Magnussen struggled to her feet with Olaf's help and began shouting in a most unladylike fashion that heads would roll, that this was an outrage, and that her attorneys would be litigating this whole 'ungodly mess' she called it.

They departed hastily and the remaining people were milling around, heads down—yabbering. The O'Malley boys for some reason thought it must be funny because they were grinning like idiots.

"So where is *Magnussen*?" said Geri—to no one in particular. The question hung in the air.

Deputy Dave McComb and Officer Barry Monkman parked in the entrance and came to place the contents of the coffin into a sealable body bag of blue plastic composition.

They had the sense to wear facemasks and latex gloves.

But the odor was unmistakable. It was the odor of death.

4

Miles Thorne was a graduate of Carnegie-Mellon in Pittsburgh.

CMU has quite a reputation for being a leading research and teaching university for Computer Science. It provides a comprehensive background in the discipline and many of its graduates go on to stellar careers in government and private industry.

Miles migrated to Massachusetts from Pittsburgh and then to Nashua, New Hampshire—where a New England variation of Silicon Valley was being established. Close to Harvard and MIT, the 1980s was a high water mark for the computer industry in New England.

Digital (DCE) was a massive player in the minicomputer age of the '70s and '80s in Massachusetts. Other successful companies like Wang and Cisco Systems showed how American innovation could reach and satisfy a worldwide market in computing technology.

Sadly, the failure to adapt to even newer microchip technology—especially the PC from both Apple and Microsoft—began to make their products too expensive and inflexible.

The development of more affordable Asian-manufactured hardware finally pulled the floor out of prices and New England's burgeoning industry just went down the drain.

Men like Miles Thorne, however, were always in demand. Although the hardware side of the industry was tanking, the software side was as robust as ever. Time has proved that software applications are the key to the computer industry in the 21st Century.

Terminology reflects that: artificial intelligence, machine learning, probabilistic networks, and so on.

Miles Thorne was able to take lofty theory and put it into practice. That earned him a reputation that—in turn—attracted a lot of attention from government and private industry.

With his Osiris Inc. startup, he built a $30,000,000 a year business that echoed the golden days of Digital and gave local municipalities hopes for thriving employment and spin-off businesses that would encourage people to settle in New Hampshire—instead of treating it like a merely seasonal tourist destination.

Delmar Robb was a seasoned computer technician with a degree in Marketing. When he first met Miles Thorne he knew he had found the proverbial pot of gold.

"This is a match made in heaven!" he used to say to Miles—meaning with Miles' programming skill and his marketing know-how, they were a perfect complement to each other.

Delmar came to believe that Miles was too introverted and his work aimed at a narrow slice of the potential market.

It was at this time that Miles was approached by the Pentagon to develop certain capabilities that would give America the edge in military and space technologies.

Miles preferred to serve his government contacts exclusively; he was doing what he loved and helping his country at the same time.

Delmar was going the other way.

He wanted to have an IPO in the same way that Apple Corp. took Steve Jobs' ideas and made them a social phenomenon—by expanding the brand exponentially.

***

Helen Watson met Miles Thorne at a conference in Boston. He was addressing scientists looking to expand our satellite program and she was running an information booth for healthcare and use of computers for data management.

It was Helen that approached him at the lunch table—but it was his choice to share that meal with her that changed everything.

"So you spend all day everyday huddled in front of a screen? Don't you like to get out once in a while?" she teased.

Miles could only grin foolishly. "That's my world and I don't really need any other," she remembered him saying. Helen made up her mind to change that.

There was something innocent about this man—something that made her want to protect him and mother him. His wardrobe, for one thing, was atrocious. His ratty beard revealed his grooming deficiencies.

Helen just reached into his little reality and stole his heart right then and there.

After a very brief courtship, Helen and Miles were married in a little church on a hill.

Bit by bit, she convinced him to step away from the corporate ambition of Delmar Robb and—on a brief honeymoon in rural New Hampshire—they discovered a charming little town called Earlsdale and bought a house there.

"How do you like it?" she said. Helen was planting flower beds in both the front and back yards. On one side was a retired couple who loved to just sit out back and enjoy every one of the 198 days of the year when the sun is shining in New Hampshire.

On the other side was a rambunctious young couple who enjoyed drinking and barbecuing in equal measures—and were unaware of their at-times outrageous behavior and lack of attire.

"Geraniums along the front border, salvia in behind," Helen decided. "The house can be so drab out front—so a little color will do just fine!"

The Thornes settled in and realized that marriage could lead to a greater happiness and contentment than they had known before.

***

On the quiet street that dead-ended around the corner in a cul-de-sac, there was no traffic and the majestic red maples that arched over the roadway gave a peculiar sense of home to this part of the community.

It was therefore quite unusual to see black SUVs parked in front of the Thorne residence on that particular afternoon.

Helen let the men in dark suits into her foyer, and then discreetly disappeared into the backyard to let her husband conduct his business with these men.

"We have been interested in your work for the Army, Mr. Thorne," the oldest man said. "We want to recruit you to do some work for *us*."

The man flipped open his ID and Miles nodded. *Central Intelligence Agency.*

"Do you work at home here?" the man asked.

"No, I have an office in the east of town, next to a warehouse. I like to keep work and family separate."

"Of course. How many people are employed there—besides you?"

"I have a couple of programmers and a secretary; that's it."

"If I lay out our proposal for you, would you be able to give us some indication as to whether this is something you could handle?" Now it was a younger fellow with a military-style haircut who spoke.

He rolled out a blueprint-sized parchment on the dining room table. Miles put on his reading glasses and pored over it for a couple of moments.

Then he said: "These stations you have marked out here...are they going to be networked?"

"That's what we want you to tell us, Mr. Thorne. Each of these stations will be centrally and remotely monitored and allow rapid response by our personnel as and when the need arises."

Miles was looking at an electronic security fence, he realized. Fences keep people out or keep people in, he reflected.

He wondered what kind of fence this was—but that thought evaporated as it was none of his business and his job was to build it—not question it.

"I'm going to need access to particular types of equipment and mechanical and electronic components," he said.

"That's not a problem, Mr. Thorne. The agency has entire departments at your disposal. We will give you clearance and access to them and—for all intents and purposes—your budget is *unlimited*."

Miles stroked his beard.

"Well, gentlemen. I think we have a deal!" Miles stood up and shook hands with all four of the agents and saw them out.

The black cars on Opal Crescent vanished like shadows in the setting sun.

5

"*Autopsy report*?" said Trace to Pete. "*Any luck?*"

"Actually, something just came in on the wire. Wanna come see it?" Pete hung up and Trace decided to walk the couple of blocks to the police station where Pete was working on his mail.

"Poisoned? He was *poisoned*?" Trace was somewhat astonished at what he was reading on the lab report.

"Makes you wonder who signed the death certificate, doesn't it? It's a fake.

Ken Covidson should have been a little more suspicious and a lot more careful when he accepted a stiff just outta the blue like that!"

"Sure, Pete, but money talks. If it weren't for the wristwatch booboo, none of this would have come to light.

Sayonara Funeral Home isn't advertising that they grab bodies off the sidewalk and throw them into a grave that may belong to just about anyone who's dead in town."

Pete McCoy scratched his chin with a sound like sandpaper on a block of maple.

"What would make someone kill this guy? With cyanide, no less?" he said.

"Just what Geri and I have been discussing," Trace said. "It's another one of those all-or-nothing situations: lots of people might have wanted him dead, but nobody jumps out at you as having a motive."

"I don't have the resources to dig into it but you know the drill: start with spouse or close family," said Pete. "Is there an insurance policy on this guy that makes him worth more dead than alive?"

"Not going to be his wife, Pete. Geri and I visited with her and she just isn't that kind, I stake my reputation on it. A woman who cooks for her husband and gets worried if he's late for dinner is not going to get her hands dirty. Next person of interest?"

"What about business partners? What do we know about his past?" Pete said.

"Not enough—apparently," Trace admitted. "Murder is extreme behavior and we need to find someone who has enough enmity or jealousy—or maybe fear about this Miles character to want to erase him.

It's not just about putting a bullet in his head and dumping him in a ditch. Someone made this very quiet and knew that once he was in the ground, the case would grow cold as a headstone and be forgotten."

"You're onto something, Trace. Maybe there's a message here: screw with us and you're gonna *disappear.*"

"Yes, Pete. Someone didn't want this in the papers. Someone wanted this to be hush-hush."

"Well, they got their wish," Pete said. "I have to go out to a farm twenty miles from here. Someone's been trespassing, so Monkman and I are gonna take a statement.

Chew on this, Trace. We need a lead."

***

Trace Edger wanted to know more about Miles Thorne.

He asked Helen Thorne if he could drop by. She said 'bring Geri'.

Seated on her sofa Helen seemed more at ease than before.

"I want to give you some background on Miles before we moved to Earlsdale.

When Miles had a successful company in Nashua. When Miles had a partner and some very clever talent in terms of engineers and programmers."

Helen slipped off her slippers and tucked her feet under her.

"I don't know what you know about him but he was one of the best! A superstar! He was one of the pioneers in Machine Learning in this country.

Naturally, he was envied and copied. The industry was in a euphoria about where computing technology was taking us.

But Miles was also quite determined to keep his operation small enough to supervise and big enough to attract contracts that paid."

"And did those contracts materialize?" asked Geri.

"Oh yes!" said Helen. "From places he hadn't thought of. The Pentagon and the CIA for instance. I remember the first time government people came to the 'shop'—as he called it.

You could feel the vibes off these people. They looked like the Men in Black!" Helen smiled.

She went on. "But you could see they were seriously interested in Miles' work and had some very specific requirements that he wasn't allowed to discuss with me.

But the money poured into the bank and Miles was content just to go on working twelve, fourteen-hour days."

"What did the partner have to say about this? Or was he partners at Osiris at that time?" said Trace.

"I think Delmar was thinking big—I mean, huge market reach and eventually going public. He was more of a marketing guy than Miles anyway. So there was a bit of tension forming there."

"Were there arguments? Disagreements?" asked Geri.

"Not at first. But you could see it was coming to a head. I could see Miles was reaching some kind of limit as the marketing aspect began to subsume the technical development side of Osiris."

"What happened then?" asked Geri.

"One day Miles came home and said 'We're leaving'.

I don't know what happened at work that day or even if it was the buildup of stress and annoyance, but Miles packed his suitcase and computers—and I loaded the SUV with a few clothes and personal items and we just drove."

"How did you end up in Earlsdale? That's quite a haul from Nashua. I'd have thought you would have gone to Boston," said Trace.

"He doesn't like the Big City—any of 'em," said Helen. "He saw this as a chance to go to the countryside and find the peace and pristine environment he really wanted.

He wanted to leave his ex-wife behind as well, I think, although we never talked about it."

"*Ex*? said Geri.

"Yeah, his first marriage was when he was young and didn't have a clue about how to be a husband and a father."

"He has kids?" asked Geri.

"""A daughter—Norma. I guess she is in her twenties now; I only met her once. She was in college at that time and the ex wanted Miles to foot all the bills—which he did.

I didn't want to interfere so I kept my mouth shut. I think Miles' will includes her somehow, though."

"You've got the will?" Trace was sitting up straight and paying attention now.

"It's somewhere," said Helen. "I haven't had the energy to dig it out yet. Might be in a safe deposit box or it might be here somewhere."

"As an attorney I specialize in wills and estate settlement, Helen. Just so you know."

"Oh? That's good. You can help me rummage through the boxes in the attic then!" Helen smiled pleasantly at Trace.

She seemed to sort of wake up and said: "Oh, I'm sorry. I haven't offered you a cup of coffee or anything!"

"That's fine, Helen," said Geri. "We won't keep you. Just wanted to get more information about Mr. Robb and his role as partner in Osiris Inc. All part of the investigation."

"Well thank you for doing all this. I'm still in shock and just bumble through the day. Please drop by again. I'm glad of the company and I promise I'll have hot coffee and cake next time!"

She gave Geri a quick hug and showed them to the door.

The noon sun shone warm and bright on the hillside and seemed to offer a note of cheer in what was turning out to be a long dreary investigation into Helen Thorne's husband's untimely death.

***

Pete met them at Danni's Diner.

"Machine learning?" said Pete like he was trying to pronounce a foreign language. "How can a machine *learn*?"

"It's a term for the merging technology of computer programming to help them inspect data in various formats and make intelligent guesses about what patterns exist in that data.

Like statistics, Pete. We know that every eight seconds a crime is committed somewhere in the United States. A machine learning algorithm can discover inferences like what kind of crime under what kind of conditions and so on."

"So we're trying to make machines as smart as a person? Is that where this is going?" Pete ordered food.

"Not necessarily," said Trace. Lawyers are experts at not giving direct answers.

"What Artificial Intelligence aims at is to do what humans do more efficiently and faster. This saves paid labor and time so that organizations can get to making decisions and taking action faster.

That may translate as less crime or shorter processing time within the criminal justice system."

"Glad I asked," said Pete drolly. "I leave that stuff up to the techies at State Police HQ. I just write parking tickets." Pete's usual breakfast meal arrived with the usual incinerated bacon strips that he loved to suck and chew on.

"We found out he has a grown daughter, Pete," said Geri. "I wonder what she might have to do with any of this skullduggery?"

"Where's she at?" said Pete.

"She lives in Manchester now and is working in CAD or something like that—something with software," Geri replied.

"Was she involved in his company—Osiris? Is that what it's called?" said Pete.

"I don't think she was," Geri said. "She was just a teenager when her parents split."

"Well, keep her on the game-board," said Pete. "She might show up later."

6

"Who else do we gotta know about?" asked Pete, once they were back in his office with the largest cup of cappuccino Beanbags offers.

"You mean like other partners we (or Helen) don't know about? Like secret partners?" Geri sipped hers.

"Well maybe like employees who felt they weren't treated well or paid enough or wanted to form a union and were refused. Usual worker bullshit," Pete explained.

"I'll have to look into it," said Trace. "At the moment I'm interested in Delmar Robb—the business partner of the dead man. They had some disagreement that busted up the cozy arrangement that they had.

I guess that often happens when a small business takes off and real money starts coming in."

"And where's he at?" said Pete slurping down the last of the sweet foamy drink.

"Down Nashua way. I need an excuse to get out of town anyway so I think I'll pay him a visit. I'll try to remember about the employee thing." Trace stood up.

"Do that!" said Pete. "I've got absolutely nothing to do but file these reports and sharpen pencils till you get back."

***

"Before you traipse off to the southern part of the state, shouldn't we have a brief search on the internet for this Robb guy?

Maybe he's in jail now." Geri snuggled into her favorite chair in Trace's office.

"LinkedIn? Facebook? Twitter? All the social media?" said Trace.

"Just Google his name and see what pops up," Geri said.

"Leads to LinkedIn," said Trace. "Let's see..." Trace was scrolling down the posting which listed Robb's education and work experience. Trace got a phone number and email.

"Belongs to the right organizations like IEEE and ICML, NeurIPS. Has his name on peer-reviewed papers. Voted 'Best New Entrepreneur in New Hampshire' in 2019."

"Okay, so he's still in the game," said Geri. "I would come but I have a story with WBZ Channel 4 that they need my input on, so I'll be in Concord for a few days."

"Well, I'll keep you posted on G-mail or G-talk then. Wish me luck!"

"Good luck, Trace. You taking your 9mm?"

"Didn't cross my mind, but maybe I should. Thanks, Geri!"

***

Trace called to set up the appointment. He was careful not to say anything more than that Miles Thorne had suddenly passed away and that—as lawyer for the estate—his job was to tie up any loose ends.

This was true for the most part. Of course, 'loose ends' can mean a lot of things.

The drive was much shorter than Trace anticipated since NH9-E and NH-101E were direct and with his Beemer tuned up recently at Pickett's Auto Service, it cost him just over $5 in gas one way.

He pulled into and registered in the Motel 66 that gave him good access to the major roads.

Established in 1746 this town now boasted 90,000 souls. New industries had replaced the computer craze of the '80s and employment was high.

Osiris Inc. had moved into more modern facilities since Miles Thorne had as a startup.

Trace's somewhat older BMW328i shared the lot with newer ones, and a host of Benzes and Audis. This company was not suffering nor were its salaried employees.

"May I have your name please, sir?" the young lady at Reception asked.

"Trace Edger. Mr. Robb is expecting me."

Delmar Robb looked like a typical midlife executive with a paunch, and manicured red beard that was showing white in the chin and throat area. He shook Trace's hand and showed him in.

“I’m not totally sure what I can help you with, Mr. Edger, but I’ll do my best. I feel bad for Helen and I want you to convey my condolences to her, will you?”

“I will indeed,” Trace replied. Then he got down to it.

“I guess what I’m hoping to learn is what in Miles Thorne’s background might give me a clue to his murder.”

“Murder? Did you say *murder*?” Robb was clearly not ready to hear that.

“That’s what the homicide detectives are telling us,” Trace said. “I will be frank with you, Mr. Robb—I want to know if there were any enemies that appeared around the time you and he went different ways.”

Robb pulled on his beard and shifted his weight in his chair.

“I can’t speak to that, Mr. Edger. We had competition—which is not the same thing. We had covert contacts in government—more than one agency, and in fact—more than one government.”

“You mean like *international* exposure?” said Trace.

“Yes. Not anyone that would be deemed hostile to American interests, but the kind of technology we offer can be very useful to nations like Taiwan or Israel who have security risks that we don’t.”

“So your company Osiris is on the radar and could have a variety of interested parties hoping to get what you have—legally or otherwise.”

"Our security is steel wire tight, Mr Edger. We vet our employees with police checks and have non-disclosure agreements. We have 24/7 security patrols on our facility.

We have some of the best anti-hacker people anywhere—people who *were* hackers who needed a regular paycheck," said Robb with a smile.

"Any employees or contractors who had a beef with Osiris? Who might have made threats to you or to Miles?"

"We hired a former East German who had intelligence experience in Stasi during the Cold War. He had a mind like a steel trap. He wasn't a computer guy—he was a security guy.

Miles caught him poking around the Cold Room—the place we keep at 42F to let the old mainframe and minicomputers stay cool since they are never powered off and put out quite a bit of heat.

Delmar started his career working on that kind of technology and since nobody knows anymore how to work it, he keeps some of our proprietary secrets on old mag tape.

Turns out that Gunter Gross knew all about that hardware since East Germany did not possess microchip technology at any time, and the Russians wouldn't give it to them.

After 1989 when the Berlin Wall came down, it was irrelevant since East Germany ceased to exist—along with the Soviet Union."

Delmar paged his assistant to bring iced tea and cookies, then continued.

"A guy in Boston I know said Gunter was admitted as a refugee and had a military background and might be a candidate for our openings in security. He was hired and all was well *until* this Cold Room escapade."

"What did he want," Trace asked. "Did he say? Did he admit he was spying?"

"No," said Robb. "He waffled and weaseled with Miles saying he just wanted to see how we implemented old hardware that he had been familiar with."

"Which Miles didn't buy," said Trace.

"Not by a long shot! Miles told me and then told me he was going to fire Gunter. He said he wanted to have him arrested but worried that would put the media spotlight on a sensitive area of our operations."

"Was there any indication that Gunter stole anything, touched or saw anything he shouldn't?" said Trace.

"Apparently not—although if he had been left alone, who knows?"

"So, this Gunter was history," said Trace.

"He evaporated," said Robb. "Just disappeared. But it was about that time that Miles started packing heat."

"*Gun*? He carried a gun with him?"

"Said he felt he was being watched or maybe even targeted. He was worth a lot and he knew it.

Personally I think that's one reason he quit Osiris.

And split to the western part of the state. To Nowheresville."

"Hey! That's my town," said Trace in mock rebuke.

"So is that where someone took him out?" said Delmar.

"Yeah. Someone who was very quiet about it. Someone professional," said Trace.

***

Back in Earlsdale, Trace asked Geri to follow up on the outcome of the lawsuit over control of Osiris that was the other part of the story why Miles left Nashua.

"Well, Miles lost. He lost his control over Osiris and had to accept that Delmar Robb was now the majority shareholder and would become the CEO.

Not long after, Robb issued an IPO and Osiris shares started trading like crazy.

Miles didn't do too badly as his privately held shares were converted to common shares and appreciated in value by quite a bit."

"So there is no reason to think that the bad blood between them led to anything more," said Trace.

"Not as far as I can see," said Geri. "You talked to the guy? What was your read on him?"

"He didn't know that Miles was murdered; I dropped that hot potato in his lap to see how he would react.

I think he was genuinely upset and surprised that someone would target his old partner."

"Any leads?"

"Yeah," Trace said. "Ex-Communist who Miles hired and caught him snooping and fired him. Name of Gunter Gross. Keep his name handy. You never know."

7

'Geri? You free for an hour? Helen Thorne has something she wants us to look at. I'll pick you up at your work. See you."

"She said she got an email, that's all I know," said Trace on the drive across town.

"Must be pretty important if she's calling you," Geri said. "You going to tell her that you spoke with Delmar?"

"I completely forgot! Yeah, I guess there's no harm in telling her. See what she says."

Trace pulled up in front of the three-story house on Opal Crescent. Although it had a driveway, Trace—out of habit—always parked at the curb. A former police lieutenant in Seattle, he never let himself get boxed in.

"How are you, Helen? No, I'll take them off." Trace and Geri were ushered into her living room.

"This time I remembered the coffee!" Helen said wheeling a cart with a silver-plated coffeepot and matching cream and sugar containers that had little feet on them like Chippendale chairs. She kept them polished and obviously considered them family treasures.

Geri blew on her cup—bone china made in England. "Good coffee!" she chirped.

"I'm so glad you could come," started Helen. "I have an email that Miles and I used for travel and recreation kinds of things. Well, I got an email this morning from some travel agency that I was not expecting."

Geri and Trace sat politely and waited for Helen to continue.

"It asked when Miles and his female friend were coming to Miami to pick up the cruise ship tickets they had ordered. They actually said: 'Your female companion.'"

"And that isn't *you*, right?" said Geri.

"It certainly isn't!" Helen replied. "I have never asked Miles to take me on a cruise and I have no real desire to go get myself stuck on a floating hotel for a week."

Trace looked at Geri and said: "So you are thinking he was cheating on you? Going off on a business trip with an unknown female?"

"Well, how would *you* call this one, Mr. Edger?"

"Did you reply to the email?" interrupted Geri.

"Not yet. I wouldn't know what to say. I didn't know what to do. So I called you."

"If you don't mind, I'll handle the email reply and see where this leads," said Trace. "If this female actually exists, she may have relationships we don't know about that may have some bearing on our case."

"Be my guest," said Helen.

"Oh, in case I forget to tell you, I made a little trip down to Nashua the other day to see Delmar Robb. Did Miles ever mention a German fellow named Gunter to you?"

"Not that I remember, no" said Helen.

"Did he ever tell you that he was concerned about his safety at work? Could that be one reason you moved to Earlsdale?"

Geri gave Trace a shocked look but quickly looked down at her cup.

"Why, no Mr. Edger. What are you implying? That someone in Osiris or connected to his work there might put him in harm's way?"

"It's just one theory I am pursuing, Helen. We cannot rule out any possibilities that may lead us to your husband's killer."

At the mention of the word 'killer' Helen burst into tears and Geri moved beside her to comfort her.

Geri gave Trace a reproachful look.

"Do you think this cruise trip was a set-up to trap my husband?" Helen said as she calmed down.

"Let me put it this way; although I did not know your husband Miles, it is certainly my impression that the man would never ever cheat on you or betray your trust in him.

So yeah—this is another mystery within the mystery we are trying to solve. One more thing to worry about."

Helen stood at the door and waved as if she were bidding goodbye to family. Geri waved back.

"When it rains—it pours," said Trace on the way back downtown.

"Good thing you are an attorney, Trace Edger. You get to play Superman and save the day!"

"Well I can't do it alone, sidekick! Can I buy you lunch? Or maybe a new car?"

They both were smiling but a thunderstorm was turning the day to night and the sky to a roiling mass of black clouds.

***

"How's this response to the Ecliptic Cruise Lines ticket office:

'*Thanks for the update, but I have moved and my plans have changed. Would you send me the details of the trip again—I have forgotten them. I will confirm new reservations once my original itinerary can be revised. With thanks, Miles Thorne.*'

I made my 'new' email address clear and that correspondence should be sent there. Let's see what the hook brings to the surface—huh, Geri?"

"Tricky, very tricky," Geri said tucking into her potato salad. "With luck, you'll get a name and then we can search for the mystery woman. Things happen for a reason—this accidental notice may be just the lead we need!"

"It doesn't make sense to *me*—so that means it was designed to mess with Miles and his family for some reason."

"How are we supposed to put the pieces together when some pieces don't even fit?" said Geri.

The rain was hammering on the roofs of cars parked along Main Street. Lightning flashed over Lake Wendigo and umbrellas were blown out as the wind howled over Lakeshore Blvd.

Geri and Trace stayed put. Danni's diner was far and away the most comfortable eatery in town and the food was superb. So they ordered dessert.

***

"So we have not asked Helen to let us look for the will, and she hasn't brought it up," said Trace.

"She said she has not tried to find it and I find that a bit curious," Geri said.

"Is there something she doesn't want anybody to find out?" said Geri. Her journalistic intuition was in the ON position.

"Could it relate to the daughter Norma?" said Trace. "We only know what Helen has told us. Maybe there was a deeper side to Miles' relationship with his daughter that she doesn't want to face."

"You don't think Norma had anything to do with Miles' death, do you Trace?" Geri looked earnestly in his eyes.

"I can't rule anything out, Geri. I don't know anymore than you do and we don't know too much at this point.

I could try and track her down in Manchester although I'm not sure what good that would do."

Marla brought the hot homemade apple pie with vanilla ice cream that Trace had requested.

"You know, ten years from now you are going to experience that pie in the 44-inch waistline you will no doubt have!" said Geri teasingly.

"But until then, Geri—" Trace licked the ice cream on the handle of the fork.

"How about this?" she said. "We both take a little jaunt down to the big city and have a visit with Norma Thorne.

If she has something to hide, we will know right away. If she does not, she can help us fill in the grey areas of the investigation. I would like to meet her, actually," Geri confessed.

"So, *tomorrow* would work?" said Trace. "My trial in Concord has been put over for a month so I just happen to be free as a bird!"

"You know, Mr. Edger, at times I get the feeling that you do very little work and spend more time with me and Pete drinking coffee and being an amateur sleuth." Geri was grinning.

"Something wrong with *that*, newspaper lady? It's how I keep my edge. That's why my name is Edger."

"Oh gawd, Trace. You need some time away. Pick me up at my condo not too early, maybe 9:30 am and in the meantime I get a GPS fix on where Miss Thorne may be hiding."

"I'll put some gas in the car and check the tires," said Trace.

***

Geri was waiting in the morning light that sparkled on the bay that was visible from her second-floor balcony on Pleasant Drive.

"I love the lake in the morning," she began. "It gives you a point of distance for your eye to focus on. I spend all my time on a laptop looking at a screen ten inches in front of my face.

I could sit all day on my balcony and look at the water. Maybe this Saturday I'll do just that!"

She continued. "Found her on LinkedIn and got her address."

"Well—*I* used the phone book and got her address," Trace said haughtily.

They both spoke at once. "*3519 Buckingham Ave., Unit 303.*"

"Good to cross-reference each other," Trace said with amusement. "Two heads are better than one."

"I think so," said Geri. "Except you are on Boundary Rd. and we haven't even stopped to get *coffee*!"

"Oh, gee—sorry, Geri. Shall I go back downtown?"

"They'll be a donut shop with coffee at a gas station somewhere on Highway 9," she said with a sigh.

"Remember you once asked me if I wanted a gun?"

She looked at the driver with head tilted slightly so she could look right in his face.

"Something's changed?" said Trace.

"I just don't feel as safe as I used to," she said. "Not since that nutbar Gary Gooseman did those prank calls and scared the bejeezus out of everyone in town!"

"Yeah, but he's in jail now."

"There will be others. Look at all the shootings in grocery stores in the news lately. Colorado, Atlanta.

Can you show me how to shoot, Trace? And pick out a nice little gun that my dainty hand can handle?"

"It would be my pleasure. Isn't your birthday coming up? I could buy you a nice little Smith & Wesson that would make you proud to own!"

"Let's go gun shopping in Manchester," she said excitedly. "Don't need more *shoes*, that's a fact!"

Trace dialed the number; Norma Thorne picked up.

In 45 minutes they were there. Manchester population-wise is ten times bigger than Earlsdale. Traffic was light for a weekday but it was nerve-wracking to negotiate left turns on signal lights.

Trace pulled up to a low-rise apartment block in an older part of the city where everything was red brick and concrete.

In Earlsdale, people made it a point to keep the wood-frame construction of older years. For the look.

Besides, there were zoning and building codes that mandated new construction to simulate the traditional New England architecture. That way, Earlsdale still looked like it was late 19th Century mock-Victorian with tudor accents on windows and walls.

The door was opened by a plain-looking young woman in jeans and a Harvard sweatshirt.

"Can I fix you some coffee?" Norma said. Geri jumped right on it. "I'll help you. I'm in major caffeine withdrawal since my ride made me come all this way without it!"

Norma laughed pleasantly and Geri decided she like her right away. She started blabbing away and complimented

Norma on her love of house plants and how did she get the jade tree to grow and not kill it like she always does.

"So...you are here because of my father? Do you know him?"

Geri's mood grew somber.

"Honey, I have some bad news for you. You Dad has passed away and your stepmom Helen doesn't know where to find you."

"No! Not my Dad! Please!" She put her head down and bawled. After a time, she blew her nose and pulled her hair back off her face.

"My step mother doesn't give two shits about me!" she said.

"My Mom and my Dad got divorced when I was sixteen and I had only gotten used to living alone with my Mom when she told me my Dad was going to remarry and leave town.

So any chance to spend quality time with him was shot to hell."

"I'm sorry you have had to go through this, Norma," Geri said.

"I'm sure many kids these days have gone through their parents' divorce but that doesn't make me feel any better," Norma said. "So does she know you are here? Did she send you to do her dirty work?"

"No, actually." Trace was speaking now. "She is still grieving the loss of your father and we are trying to help her put the pieces together.

We need to ask you a few uncomfortable questions," he said.

"You don't have to answer—we're not police officers or social workers. I'm an attorney and I will be handling the execution of your father's will—I believe he did leave a will. Geri is a freelancer who is my partner when I need an extra pair of ears and eyes."

Trace asked for another cup; Norma obliged.

"Were you aware of any problems your father might have been having with people—both before and after he moved to Earlsdale?"

"Is his death somehow related to that? Is that where this is going?" Norma's eyes and words were hot and cold at the same time.

"That's not what I'm saying. But there was a lot of money flowing through his company and after he left his partner Delmar kind of shut him out in the cold. Or at least that's my sense of it."

"I remember him," Norma said. "He was all about 'selling the product' and going for a global market or something."

"Yes, I've spoken with him," Trace admitted. "But he held no ill will toward Miles that I could see."

"I didn't know the inside story of my father's business dealings, Mr. Edger. I was just pissed at him for leaving me and my Mom. He gave us money but that's not the point."

"Do you remember him saying he would leave you something in his will?" said Trace gently.

"He never said anything about a will or a trust or any such thing that I can recall. I can't ask my real Mom because she and her new husband won't talk to me."

"I'm sorry you've had problems," said Trace.

"Yeah, it's been rough. I threw my last boyfriend out cause he was allergic to getting gainful employment after college.

So it's just me and Muffy."

She opened the bathroom door and a white ball of fluff shot into the room and put her little paws up on Trace's pant leg.

Trace patted her as her little pink tongue licked his fingers like he was fried chicken.

Norma picked her dog up and placed her on her lap.

"So if you find the will, what will happen?" said Norma.

"You mean what will happen if you are a *beneficiary*," Trace said.

"I think the man owes me something, don't you?" she said bitterly.

"Not for me to say, but I *will* say that if I can locate the will and get it to probate court and *if* there is provision made for you, then I will do everything in my power to see that you get what's coming to you."

Sometimes Trace had a way of speaking with authority that made people pay attention.

"I would be grateful, Mr. Edger, for that. I'm glad you took the time and effort to find me. At least someone knows I'm alive. You have my number. Let me give you my e-mail."

Geri and Trace bade goodbye to Miss Thorne and got back on the highway west—just in time for rush hour—which cost them an extra 45 minutes getting home.

Trace dropped Geri at the corner convenience store and promised to meet over coffee in the morning.

The storm of the day before had left puddles that splashed as Trace made his way down the street and over to his apartment not far from his office on Main St.

In this part of the country—when stars came out—they really shone brightly. Trace could see the Big Dipper and follow its bowl to The North Star. It made him feel peaceful. For a moment.

8

In the modern world, privacy is a thing of the past. As we reveal our identities and lives on social media, there are those who would exploit that and cause us harm.

But when that threat comes, how many of us are ready to deal with it?

It was late afternoon and Penny was putting on her sweater and drying the few dishes she had washed in the kitchenette of Trace Edger's law office when the call button on the desk phone lit up.

She put the call through.

"*Trace Edger*?" the attorney said.

The voice was a woman's voice—not a native speaker of English since there was an Eastern European accent.

"Stop what you are doing, Mr. Edger. This is not any of your business. Stop looking. Stop asking questions."

Click. The call ended as quickly as it began.

Trace called Geri; she hustled over just as Penny was locking the office door on her way out.

Saying goodnight to her, Geri threw open the inner door where Trace spent his days and closed it firmly and sat down.

"A woman? A secret admirer?" Geri was trying to lighten the mood but unsuccessfully.

"At least she knows my name!" said Trace. "She also seems to know my 'business' and wants me to butt out of hers!"

"She obviously feels threatened by our investigation," said Geri. "Which means we are getting *warmer*.

Let me see—you went to Nashua to see *Delmar*, we went to Manchester to see *Norma*. We have been to see *Helen* at least twice.

Which of these actions made some strangers begin to worry about what we are up to?"

"It also suggests Miles has stirred up some hornet's nest that we don't know about yet.

What could Miles have known or been doing that would result in his murder?

And in this threat that I got just now?" Trace said.

"Whatever it was, it must be connected to one or more of the people we have paid a visit to.

We must have been followed, or one of those people said something to somebody and that somebody is pointing their finger right at us!" Geri said, shifting the chair away from the window and pulling the roller blind right down to the top of the radiator.

She continued. "Maybe we'd better get me that gun after all!"

"Guns won't keep us safe if these people really want to make trouble for us," Trace said. "They have no compunctions about eliminating obstacles to their ambitions."

"So let's go back to Miles Thorne and what he had going," Trace said. "Must be something to do with his work."

"Computers? Artificial Intelligence? That's a mighty big playground, Trace. Can we narrow it down?"

Geri wanted to smoke but she needed to resist. It took months of struggle to quit and every quitter knows it just takes one cigarette to be right back where you started.

She dug an emery board out of her bag and started to file in a compulsive way—just to keep her hands busy.

"Delmar said Miles had military contracts with the Feds. Whatever Miles had it must have been attractive enough to get Washington to pay attention.

I don't think it was a hardware thing though. That's wide open and lots of chips and boards are made in China or Korea now.

It's gotta be a software suite that does something unique and powerful. Maybe an algorithm that no one else thought of before," Trace was saying.

"And could get you *killed* if someone wanted it bad enough," said Geri.

"Or wanted to keep it from falling into other hands.

This voice on the phone could have been someone from any one of a dozen former Soviet satellite states.

It doesn't take too much imagination to understand that Russian intelligence operatives might like to get these secrets too!" Trace said.

"Are we going to get killed, Trace?" Geri was blowing fingernail dust all over her outfit.

"If they wanted us dead—they wouldn't have bothered to call, Geri."

***

"But why *murder*, Trace? Why didn't they just *kidnap* him and take him to Bora-Bora or someplace and squeeze him for information?"

Geri had convinced Trace she felt safer in Beanbags Cafe across the street—and she needed a double shot espresso right away.

"He might have resisted. Or they might have seen that the CIA had tabs on him and there was little chance to grab Miles from under their noses and run," Trace said.

"Pete still thinks it's the wife. Or the cruise ship babe!" said Geri.

"We're a little deeper in than *that* now," said Trace gloomily.

"Should we get Pete to put a watch on Helen? She could be in danger and she wouldn't have a clue!"

"Yeah, I hear you Geri. With exactly four uniformed cops in this town of eleven thousand, the Chief can hardly spare one to do a stakeout on a 'maybe' or a 'could be'."

Geri piped up. "Hey, what if some...person or organization hit on Miles and maybe Miles was going to offer them something—and then they got paranoid that Miles would rat them out to the FBI so they bumped him off?"

"Throw it on the pile, kiddo," said Trace. "There has to be one possibility that is more likely that all the others if we could just discern it. It could be staring us in the face. Hidden in plain sight. But if we don't have that one clue—."

"Remember Edward Snowden?" said Geri. "The CIA computer geek who blew the whistle on the security apparatus in this country—then fled to Hong Kong and eventually Russia?"

"What about him?" said Trace.

"What if Miles Thorne was going to do a '*Snowden*'? What if he was going to reveal secrets which threaten our national security but they got to him before he could escape?"

"That would line up with the stealthy manner in which he was killed: dead and buried so to speak."

Trace ordered an oat bar—one of his favorite Beanbags treats-- relatively low in sugar and fat.

"Where are all his files?" said Geri. "Where does—I mean '*did*'—he keep his hard drives or CDs or however he stored stuff? Or maybe some on *hard copy*?

I know you and me both keep a lot of sensitive information on plain paper, in manila envelopes or file folders in good old-fashioned metal filing cabinets."

"That's a question I've been meaning to ask myself—but you beat me to it, Geri!"

"Doesn't he have an office in town? If he worked at home then Helen wouldn't be waiting up for him every night with dinner ready," Geri speculated.

"Good point. Why didn't we think of that earlier?" said Trace.

"Cause we've been too busy chasing down boogeymen to pay attention to the ordinary," said Geri.

9

"You guys are blowing this whole thing waayyy out of proportion," Pete said.

"If you don't think it's the wife, or the daughter—fine. Then it's the funeral director guy with the disease name."

"Covidson," said Trace.

"Yeah—*that* guy! He's got a good little racket going where he handles all the deceased in town, embalms them, sells the family a fancy casket with flowers, a headstone—by the time John Doe is in the ground, this Covidson has raked in ten, twenty grand!" Pete said.

"Jealous?" said Geri in her typical teasing way.

"You bet I am!" said Pete with feeling. "If I had any brains, I would've got into the funeral business instead of the policing business. Could've retired by now!"

"So what would *his* motive be for just randomly killing Miles Thorne?" Trace said.

"Are you stunned? Have more coffee, my attorney brother!" said Pete. "Did I not make myself *clear* enough? The money!

Let's say *three* people a week—I'm exaggerating here—die in Earlsdale.

They gotta take the body to Sayonara Funeral Services who arrange to place the unfortunate person into a grave across the street in the cemetery—that they just happen to own!"

Pete was on a roll.

"*Three* times *four* times *twelve*—minus a couple of weeks where no one passes away—and whaddya got?

Multiply that by *ten thousand dollars a burial*—I'll low-ball it—one million, four hundred and forty thousand dollars—and that's your *yearly income,* my dear fellow!"

Pete was pink in the face and starting to sweat under his police hat so he took it off.

Everyone in the diner started to clap for Pete so he briefly rose and took a bow.

"You make a mighty convincing case," admitted Trace. Geri was just grinning like a baboon.

"Well, you keep an eye on that Sayonara Funeral Home, Pete," said Trace finally. "Don't let them out of your sight. You're right! everybody that *dies* here—*lies* here. In our cemetery.

With the watchful eye of the law right there, nobody is going to pull any more fast ones in Earlsdale!"

Trace paid for his friends and they hit the sidewalk in buoyant spirits.

"Did I tell you the good news?" Pete said just as they were splitting up.

"Mayor Han called. She had just spoken to the city accountant. She has the money to buy us a brand-spanking-new police vehicle. An *SUV,* no less!

We pick it up at Pickett's Wednesday. He will put in heavy duty shocks and springs, wire up the siren and lights. All the bells and whistles!"

"Congratulations, Pete!" said Geri—briefly hugging the Chief of Police.

"You don't let your men drive it—it's just for *you*, Pete!" she teased.

"Damn right!" said Pete. "I'm gonna park the Charger in back. Just ticked over 300,000 miles that baby.

Maybe they'll be a *real* emergency one of these days and I can show up in a *proper* police car!"

With that, Pete headed back to his precinct house on First and Karen—and Geri and Trace to their own offices on Main St.

***

Trace called to check. "*How's the new SUV, Pete? It's a GMC did you say? Great. Don't forget to put some gas in the tank.*"

Trace was finishing up some work at his desk. Geri breezed in like she owned the place.

"Hello, Sunshine!" she said, brandishing a mocha java in Trace's direction.

"Pete got his new police vehicle," Trace reported. "He's like a kid with a new toy!"

"He's waited bloody years for this!" said Geri. "It's about time!"

"So when are we going to ask Pete for the warrant to search Miles' old office?" Trace said.

"As soon as he comes down off his high about the SUV," Geri answered. "Don't spoil it for him by making him apply to the judge in Concord for a search warrant. He hates filling those in.

Have to *name the premises*, state what the *probable cause* for the entry and search is, state *exactly* what items therein are to be searched or seized. Oh I *know*!"

"We can make it easier for him if we just go out there and peek in the windows. Tell him what needs to be searched in order to expedite this homicide investigation," said Trace.

"Okay, later. After dark. It's Meatloaf Special Night at Danni's Diner and I know we don't want to miss it!" Geri said dabbing some lipstick on.

"C'mon, Trace!" She tugged his arm as they exited to the street and turned left going southbound past the jeweller's, the bakery, and the shoe store. Orange light fell on the windows as dusk was approaching.

***

"Gawd—that meatloaf is to die for!" Geri exulted as they breathed in the warm evening air outside the diner.

Danni's didn't close till eleven which meant Daniela herself mainly—since she was single—had to stay past midnight to clean up and put food away and garbage out.

She did it all cheerfully—and took home food to her aging mother in the Italian community where they lived near Second between Tom and Harry St.

Pete was in the cab of the GMC with Dave McComb, Barry Monkman and Danno McFee.

They were busy getting the interior of the vehicle broken in with crumbs and sauce from a fast-food joint off Commerce and South Main St. when the 911 call came in on the police radio.

"*Chief McCoy*?" the female dispatcher sounded staticky on the speaker.

"*We have a fire at a warehouse and office out near Boundary Road. Can you get your Fire Department on it? Do you think you will need assistance from Keene or Hillsborough*?"

"I won't know until I get there," said Pete into his mic. He turned his head to his passenger.

"Dave, get John on your cell and tell him we have a fire. He will alert his volunteer team. Make sure you tell him Boundary Road past Revere Road. Not far from the driving range."

Pete switched on his lights and siren and peeled out onto Hwy. 9 East and the adrenaline was pumping!

The fire station was right beside the police station on First Ave. Volunteers numbered about twelve on a good day. They all had day jobs and some even worked for the City.

'Volunteers represent the spirit of America' Trace once said. 'Men and women with courage and moral belief in doing what is right are what built this country from a wilderness and rag-tag group of colonies into 'one nation under God'.

Pete knew that all across the United States there are small bands of courageous volunteers who assist in fire fighting in their community and do so only for the benefit of that community and its citizens—whether in towns like Earlsdale or in rural settings and small towns in the vast expanse of land all the way to the Rockies and beyond.

By the time Pete reached the blaze, he knew no efforts of the firefighters would save the building. It was gone.

The fire truck pulled in and set a perimeter to control the flames and hot cinders. The steel skeleton of the low-rise office and adjacent warehouse stood alone amid the smoking debris and devastation.

Pete called Trace. He needed someone he could trust to help sort this out.

"You know *this* was the office I needed a search warrant for?" said Trace squinting as the acrid smoke shifted with the wind.

"So this has to be an arson," said Pete. "Not an accident, not a natural fire—but a deliberately-set fire."

"If that's so," Trace said, "first thing is to look for point-of-origin. And get a read on whether an accelerant was used.

I'm thinking arson, to—because this was a very hot fire—in order to do *this* kind of damage in a relatively short period of time. Accelerant-fueled fires burn twice as hot as fires that just burn framing and random materials inside the structure."

"So that's the *what*; what about the *who*?" said Pete.

"Honestly, I think someone who knew that Miles Thorne's office was going to get searched and wanted to destroy incriminating evidence before that happened."

"This makes me nervous, Trace. This is an escalation of violence that we don't see around here. This is mobsters or gang-related—I don't know. Or at least someone who is desperate enough to go to these lengths to foil law enforcement.

But why? A computer guy gets snuffed and it looks like a professional hit job. But then the *call you got* and then *this*—it's getting out of hand. What do they *want*?"

"They want us to butt out," Trace said.

"What I don't get is why they torched the place? Isn't that being a little too obvious?" Pete said.

"Why not pull a minor burglary to remove Thorne's files and hardware—if it poses such a risk to their operation?"

"All good questions, Pete. My feeling is that they are sending us a message.

They are flexing their muscles so we will be intimidated and back off the case. Just like the woman on the phone call to me."

"So what do we do next?" said Pete.

"We wait."

10

"You know, Geri, I think we have to put a little more pressure on Helen to find that will."

Trace Edger was flipping through the newspaper until he found Geri's story about the fire. He quickly looked it over and put the paper down.

"We also need to see if Miles had insurance on that building," he said. "Helen would be the beneficiary of that policy—but we need to see if there's someone *else*. Someone who needed money."

"Helen wouldn't do a thing like that," said Geri. "Too obvious and too out of character."

"I agree. Let's not assume this fire was *not* set for the insurance—although that is a typical reason for arson. 75% of arson in the United States is related to insurance and related fraud.

No, this fire was targeted at the contents of the building—not the building itself. Someone wanted Miles to be out of business—as if *dead* were not enough!"

"There has to be something valuable that Miles left behind," said Geri. "Something that—like Miles himself—is best destroyed completely. Like a secret."

"Yeah. Like a secret. Miles' work is all about secrets. And let's say that torching the office removed the threat that the files and notebooks for good, will we have peace and quiet now?" said Trace.

"That's anybody's guess," said Geri. "Let's go back to what you said at the beginning. We need to find Miles' will.

There could be any number of surprises there. I'm not quite certain why Helen hasn't jumped on it—for the money, if nothing else."

"That's true," said Trace. "She can't live on her savings or credit for very long. Assuming she has a mortgage like everybody else, she is going to need what's in that will!"

"So why don't we take Mrs. Thorne out for dinner—somewhere classy—like Tony's. Loosen her up with a glass of chablis and see where that takes us."

"I could use a glass of chablis myself, Geri. Let me call her and see what she says."

***

"I must say I feel flattered that you would invite me for an evening out," said Helen climbing into the right rear passenger seat.

"We always come to your house, so it's time you got out and stretched your legs a bit," said Geri in a friendly upbeat tone.

"I just never think of that—I guess I'm still processing Miles' death," she said.

Trace saw his opening.

"Speaking of Miles, we were wondering whether you had managed to put your hands on his will. You had mentioned that it might be in a safety-deposit box at the bank."

"Why, I'm two steps *ahead* of you, Mr. Edger. Here it is right *here*!"

Helen drew a tan-colored envelope from her handbag and passed it to Geri.

"We can have dinner first and then—at a more private location like my office—examine the document. You are thinking along the lines that I am," Trace said. "By the way, do you like Italian food?"

Trace parked in the side lot and escorted his companions inside. As luck would have it, the owner Tony Barone was speaking with his guests in a very full and noisy milieu.

Tony smiled and extended his hand.

"Mr. Edger. Always a pleasure. Ciao, ladies. I'm Tony and I'm pleased to make you welcome to my little cafe."

He found a table off in a sheltered corner and seated his guests.

"Drinks are on me!" he said with his native Italian exuberance.

Geri spoke up. "Do you have Chablis?"

For a moment, Tony frowned playfully.

"Chablis is French, *signora*. My place is authentic Italiano—we prefer reds in Italy and I have a valpolicello from my hometown in Tuscany that will melt your heart!"

"We'll be delighted to try it, Tony," Geri responded. Tony rushed off to his kitchen, stopping here and there to greet customers.

Tony's Bistro was very, very popular in Earlsdale. Weekends were reservation only and always full until past midnight.

His Italian chefs could do any pasta whose name you couldn't pronounce—and did a fabulous job with fresh seafood trucked in from Portsmouth.

Mandi brought the wine.

"Hello again, Mr. Edger." She seemed genuinely glad to see him. She gave a warm smile to Geri and Helen.

She uncorked the bottle with flair and poured two fingers into Trace's glass.

He smelled, he tasted, he raved. Mindi poured for the ladies and left the bottle securely in a basket beside the table.

She brought fresh bread and a dish of antipasto and olives. Helen was looking around with satisfaction and seemed to be enjoying the moment.

"This wine has no bite," she said. "It's smooth and has a hint of cherry. I love it!"

"Cheap wines have bite," said Geri matter-of-factly. "Good wines soothe the palate."

"The cherry flavor is probably a small percentage of grenache which is typical in Europe—even Italy," said Trace with a wink.

Geri had to scold Trace for filling up on bread and antipasto while waiting for the main course.

"It's so the wine doesn't hit me so hard," he lied.

Dinner was a three-course extravaganza with soup, salad, and pasta. Trace had fettuccine alfredo; Helen had veal parmagiana, and Geri had ravioli made fresh that day.

Mandi brought another bottle of red, and the three just ate and drank themselves into a very pleasant mood indeed.

When Helen went to the ladies' room, Geri asked Trace if he thought she knew about the fire.

"I doubt it somehow," he said. "If she does—I want her to bring it up. I don't want to be the bad-boy attorney who spoils the evening with a dose of reality."

Helen returned with a slight look of puzzlement on her face.

"Everything alright?" asked Geri.

"Yes. Fine. I think so. I saw a woman in there I thought I recognized.

She's the wife of the jerk next door—Randy Miserly. Not sure why she avoided me. Maybe she heard about Miles."

"Did Miles know these people?" said Geri.

"I don't think so. They move in a different crowd," Helen said with a touch of disdain.

Geri and Trace saw a young attractive woman emerge and go to sit with a man about ten years older at a nearby table.

"That her?" whispered Geri. Helen nodded and downed the last of her glass.

"And that scuzzy guy she's with? Her husband?"

Helen smirked.

Trace handed his credit card to Mandi who asked if everyone had enjoyed their meal.

The three stepped into the dampish night air and Trace drove down the twisting canyon road to the downtown, then mounted another incline to get Helen home.

She fished in her purse for her key.

"Thank you so much!" she said. "I really enjoyed that."

Trace noted she had the presence of mind to leave the front porch light on. He wondered if she had a security alarm and made a mental note to ask her.

He pulled up on Pleasant Drive outside the condo. "Well, Geraldine? Have fun tonight?"

"I did, Trace, thank you! Call me in the morning. Here—take the will. We can look at it tomorrow."

Trace let the envelope lie on the seat like a mystery guest that would soon speak words of importance.

The last thing Trace remembered was switching off the bedside lamp. Then, it was morning.

***

Geri brought coffee. Penny offered fresh-made muffins with blueberries—her specialty. Trace was on the phone to Helen, then to the taxi company to pick her up.

"I love how your muffins are not too sweet," Geri said to Penny. "What's your secret?"

Penny laughed and said: "Brown sugar."

"Helen's on her way," said Trace helping himself to the biggest muffin on the plate.

"I'll get a draft letter for the Probate Court ready," said Penny. "I think we can make the 2:00pm pickup by the courier."

Penny was the soul of efficiency. Without her innate sense of organization, the lawyer would be completely lost—buried in paper and swamped with phone calls.

At length, footsteps on the stairs announced Helen's arrival.

Penny took her coat as she entered the inner chamber of the law office.

"Have you opened it?" she said breathlessly, reaching for a muffin.

"Waiting for you," said Trace. "More courtesy than legality."

"Well let's get to it!" Helen said with enthusiasm.

Geri noticed that Helen had rouged her cheeks and wore lipstick. The thought crossed her mind that a fairly young and reasonably attractive woman like this would not remain single for too long.

Being divorced herself, Geri had made up her mind long ago to keep men at a comfortable distance. In fact, she had not dated anyone for over five years and if you asked her she would say she hardly noticed.

Geri was working as an investigative journalist for both the local paper and talk radio station—with occasional sound bites for the TV station WMUR an ABC affiliate in Concord and Manchester.

As if that were not enough, she was developing the investigative side of her work more and more—partnering with Trace Edger—a lawyer with a penchant for putting his own nose into local crime, all with the blessing of Pete McCoy, Chief of Police.

"Have you looked at this, Helen?" said Trace with a note of excitement in his voice.

"Nope. It is as I gave it to you—unopened, unsealed since Miles finished it."

"Well, there's good news and bad news—but the good news is you are generously provided for and can certainly pay off your mortgage and sundry debts," said Trace.

Helen looked mournful. "Miles loved me," she said. "I know that. I know he would want me to be okay."

"Seven-figure 'okay'," said Trace. "Once we evaluate his estate as an entirety, I'm thinking quite a few million dollars will find a home in your bank account."

Geri piped up.

"It's funny how many women have no idea of their husband's net worth," she said. "Men just stash money away in the darnedest places and say tickety-boo to their spouses about it.

Of course, equal numbers of husbands leave a sizeable debt for their wives to deal with, too," she added.

"So what is the next step, Mr. Edger," Helen asked.

"You hire me as the executor and I file this with Probate Court so that they are satisfied that its provisions accord with law and with the intentions of the testator.

Once that process ends—about ten weeks from now—we can crack a bottle of champagne and drink to your good health!" said Trace with a smile.

"You two have been such a help to me," Helen admitted. "I know I have nothing to worry about."

"About last night..." said Geri. "These neighbors of yours—you suggested there was some monkey-business that involved them. Do you want to elaborate on that?"

"I can't point my finger at anything in particular," Helen began. "It's as much my woman's intuition as anything. But that woman seemed to be flirting with Miles over the fence in the backyard on a number of occasions.

The weird thing is that her husband Randy was sitting right there. He would drink beer and watch baseball on a small TV on a cart.

Carly would flounce around their pool in a bikini and make a spectacle of herself as if movie agents were lurking in the bushes just waiting to sign her to a contract."

Geri shot a look at Trace—who shrugged.

"What was your husband's response to her behavior?" said Geri.

Miles just laughed it off. He liked yard work because it was physical—because it took his mind away from the endless flow of thoughts that dominated his daily work.

I don't think he gave her more than an occasional nod. He never spoke to them and he never spoke to me about them.

That tells me they were insignificant and I never gave it another thought."

"Until this Ecliptic Travel agent called," said Trace. "Do you think this might have been a prank? The neighbors taking things a little too far?

Because I followed up on that reservation by e-mail. The name of the woman on the cruise itinerary was Carly Miserly. They had a scan of her passport," Trace said.

"So you think she was trying to seduce my husband by starting an affair on some cruise ship?" Helen's voice rose sharply.

"I think these people are sharper than they look," said Trace. "They must have known your husband was a successful businessman and that blackmailing him might yield a little cash settlement so long as it worked out and nobody was the wiser."

"That little slut!" shouted Helen. "I knew she was up to something. Her—and that creep, Randy!"

"We all agree that Miles was unlikely to run off with her or give in to their potential threat; do you think it is possible they might have turned on Miles and....caused him harm?" Trace looked right at her.

"What a question!" said Helen. "Let me collect myself. Geri, could you get me a coffee?"

Helen sat and sipped thoughtfully. At length she spoke.

"I don't think so, Mr. Edger. I think these people are low-life trash—but murder is one huge step outside their sandbox.

Besides, what would it gain them? I think they like to mess with people—but only to a point."

"Okay," said Trace. "Let's leave it at that for now. With any luck, the estate can be distributed by month end. Until then, keep your front door locked and your alarm system functioning.

Oh—I meant to ask you—you do have a security alarm, right?"

"Miles insisted on it," Helen said. "Close circuit TV in specific areas, as well. I sleep better knowing it's there."

"So will we. I'll call you a cab. Stay in touch, Helen."

11

"Are you gonna show me how to shoot this thing? Or I am gonna get Pete to do it?"

Geri was trying out the heft and grip of her new pistol.

"It's heavy!" she said. "How am I supposed to carry this around? I need stronger straps on my purse."

"A holster, silly," said Trace. "Hip holsters can be very stylish. We can choose real leather or go with ripstop nylon and velcro."

"Whatever works. This must a good two, three pounds with a clip in," she said.

"The price of protection, honey! This is the trigger; don't touch it until you're ready to shoot something.

This is the safety; keep it on until you're ready to touch the trigger."

Trace showed her how to use the safety button and how to put the magazine in and out.

"Let's go shoot some bottles on the weekend. There are some key pointers that will need to be followed and it's best if we use live ammo for that."

***

"What's the story on the arson, Pete?" Trace had dropped by the station with cappuccinos in hand.

"As we suspected—it was done by pros, or least it *wasn't* done by amateurs.

Fire marshal in Concord said his men found traces of diesel fuel and an unidentified substance in several areas that had burned faster and left deeper charring in the framing."

"This helps us in one way and hurts us in another," said Trace.

"Say!" said Pete enjoying his favorite drink from his favorite chair.

"It's bad because whoever did this was careful and left few clues. It's good in the sense of it helps us narrow down the candidates for Miles' homicide.

In other words, the murder and the fire are related. We are not dealing with someone with a grudge or an axe to grind over something Miles did or didn't do."

"So whoever is behind this is a big fish, is that what you're saying?"

"A great white shark!" said Trace.

"What was it Roy Scheider in *Jaws* said to Robert Shaw? 'You're going to need a bigger boat!'"

Both men laughed heartily. Then Pete got a serious look on his face.

"Are we in over our head here, Trace? Isn't it time we put in a call to the FBI?"

“The only difference between us and the Bureau is that they have more information and a much bigger budget,” said Trace.

“Right now we could use more information, Trace,” said Pete. He took his feet off the desk and squirmed in his chair. “Maybe more guys with guns!” he added.

“Problem with the Feds is that they take over the case and that will make a lot of smoke and noise and our killer or killers will slither back into the swamp.

We’re getting close, Pete, I can feel it. That’s why the phone calls, that’s why the fire. They sense that we’re onto them—and I’m guessing they are making the classic mistake of thinking we know more than we *do*.

We have to keep them thinking that—let the sweat run down the small of their backs.”

“You mentioned to me about some guy named Sam Screed after you got back from Nashua,” Pete said.

“Delmar Robb dropped that one in my lap on my way out,” said Trace. “He knows that Sam Screed approached Miles after Miles bailed out of Osiris.

He was thinking Screed wanted to put together a deal with Miles Thorne that would get some serious cash flowing into both their pockets.”

“Screed *knew* people?” said Pete. “I mean...*legit* people?”

“That I don’t know,” said Trace. “But I’m guessing that men like Miles Thorne are seen as cash cows who won’t be spending much time alone in the pasture.

Money can buy lots of things but it can't buy the kind of raw genius that was Miles Thorne. You have to set up a situation that will tempt your little software wizard into sharing his discoveries."

"So why don't we do a little digging around to see where this Screed character is at and maybe pay him a visit?" Pete suggested.

"Why don't we?" said Trace.

***

When Trace got back to his office it was close to noon.

"You have a client waiting in your office," said Penny. "Mrs. Thorne!" she whispered.

"Morning, Helen," said Trace as he swept into his office and closed the door.

"Mr. Edger, I'm frightened!" Helen Thorne half-stood and then sat and fidgeted and looked out the window as if she thought someone might we watching her here.

"What happened?"

"I was getting ready for bed. I was in my nightie. My bedside phone rang and I picked it up." She leaned into the desk and dragged her chair with one hand.

"The caller said that I was being foolish in trying to find out what happened to my husband. They said what's done is done. For my own well-being, I should drop the matter altogether.

Then they said the worst thing of *all*—they said '*we are watching*'."

"They said *we*?"

"Yes, *we* are watching. They didn't say what for.

I feel like I'm taking my life in my hands just coming here. That's why I left the car at home and took a taxi.

Isn't this something the police should be aware of?" Helen said.

"They didn't ask for money or threaten you with harm?"said Trace.

"No. But they didn't have to; I'm sure they know I'm just a woman living alone. I don't even want to go home—thinking someone is outside peering in my windows, watching my every move. It's like a Hitchcock movie."

"Until we know this isn't just some crackpot playing a prank or harassing you—we need some clear evidence that criminal activity is at play before the police can get involved," Trace said.

"They burned down my husband's office to the ground! Isn't that criminal *enough*?" Helen's eyes flashed.

"We can't say for sure if the phone call you received is in any way related to the arson," Trace said soothingly. "Miles had apparently made some enemies along the way but there is no logical reason why they should come after you—especially now that Miles is out of the picture."

Helen Thorne just sat as if too deep in thought to move.

"Let's be a bit more discreet about our meetings then," said Trace. "I have to see you as soon as the Probate Court has finished its review and released the will back to me. I'll stay on it.

Just try not to feel you are a prisoner in your own home. You said you don't have any family here. Is there anyone you could stay with for a while?"

"I wouldn't want to put anyone in danger," she said. "I'll just set the alarm and cameras and leave all the outside lights on for the time being."

"Call me if you need me; here's my private number. I'm sure nothing's going to happen. They just want to scare you."

"Well, they did a *darned good job*!" said Mrs. Thorne.

12

As soon as Helen Thorne had left Trace dialed Geri for a late lunch at the Diner.

"Who do you think it is, Trace? I mean who do you *really* think it is?"

"Someone who has a lot to lose if we find out more about Miles' secret contacts," Trace said. "I think we can pretty much rule out the wife, the daughter, the former partner and the loony neighbors."

"So, Big League players, then."

"This is industrial espionage, Geri.

Either the Good Guys or the Bad Guys are trying to obliterate Miles Thorne and his software. Maybe both sides!"

"What if they cross paths with each other along the way?" Geri asked.

"Then expect trouble!" Trace admitted. "How we got in the middle of all this still amazes me.

A superstar computer programmer moves to our community then gets himself snuffed. Leaving us to pick up the pieces," Trace said.

Breakfast arrived and both of them ate ravenously. 'When you live alone, you sometimes forget to cook,' Trace once said.

"So who's left on our list of suspects?" said Geri. "Would it do any good to put some heat on Ken Covidson?"

"I doubt it," said Trace. "I think he knows the minimum he needs to—to get paid.

Whoever did the hit knows that Covidson accomplished what he was paid to—put a body in the ground as quietly as possible. And I think they think that Covidson is going to be blamed for incompetence at least—and professional negligence at worst. Look at the Magnussen affair!"

"They said they are watching Helen Thorne, which suggests to me they are watching all of us, Trace!

They must know Miles was exhumed and his body sent for analysis. They know there will be question marks," Geri said.

"I just had a brilliant idea—evil--but brilliant! said Trace, ordering more coffee.

"Oh, I like this about you Trace! You're squeaky clean but you know how to stir up dirt when the occasion calls for it!"

"If we came up with a suspect in the murder of Miles Thorne, the real perpetrators will think we have made a big enough mistake for them to get away with this. Then the phone calls and fires and threats will all go away," said Trace.

"So if they are thinking we have goofed up the investigation—so they let their guard down—that gives us an opening to get to the core of this whole business. They won't see us coming!" Geri said bouncing in her chair.

"That's the idea, Geri. But it'll require the full cooperation of the police and the prosecutor.

At present, the public does not know anything more than Miles Thorne died suddenly from a heart attack.

The only persons who know it was murder is *us*—and the murderers *themselves*!

***

Trace paid a visit to his pal and Earlsdale Chief of Police—Peter 'Pete' McCoy.

"I have an idea I want to share with you, Pete."

Trace explained what he had just discussed with Geri.

"There's only one problem with that, Trace," Pete said.

"Sam Screed was charged with second-degree murder over three weeks ago and is in custody awaiting trial. He didn't make bail."

"*Murder*? Well how convenient! See, Pete, if we piggyback another homicide on top of the one he's in jail for already, it suits our purposes nicely!

Sam Screed is going down for murder *anyways*—so he could be charged for Miles' murder *as well* and later—after the first trial is over—the DA can drop the second charge for lack of evidence.

And if we are very, very lucky—we will have our bad guys in our net by then."

"Is this what attorneys *do* all day? Sit around and dream up crime scenarios?" said Pete with a grin.

"Only when we are bored. So what do you *think*?" Trace went on.

"We claim that Screed made a threatening call to Miles' widow—which gives us probable grounds to suspect he may have killed Miles—and that gives the DA enough to pin a second homicide on him.

The *Concord Monitor* will pick the story up—and the right people will read it—and we're away to the races!"

"Maybe he *was* the guy who called Helen Thorne and gave her the heebie-jeebies!" said Pete.

"Maybe," said Trace.

***

"This arrived by courier, Mr. Edger. I think it's what you've been waiting for!"

Penny Lane—Trace Edger's secretary and Girl Friday lifted a heavy paper package onto her desk.

She was the only thing standing between him and Chaos, Trace often remarked. Penny knew where everything was and what went where and by what date. In a word, she was the ultimate organizer!

"This is the Thorne will," he said gloating. "Now we'll see who gets what.

Penny? Can you put it a call to Helen Thorne and ask her to come downtown—say—midmorning tomorrow?"

Trace texted Geri to get her butt over to his office ASAP. She brought treats.

"As it turned out," Trace was saying, "the Court has approved most of the terms of the Last Will and Testament of Miles Gerald Thorne—except one.

They have noticed that a substantial number of shares in Osiris Inc. along with $50,000 in cash were left to 'My precious princess...'."

"And they don't know who that is, right?" said Geri.

"You know—this reminds me of a famous English case from a hundred years ago where the farmer died after having his tractor topple over and crush him," Trace began.

"Ewww! That's nasty!" said Geri.

"He scratched three words in the fender paint as he lay dying: 'All to Mother'.

This is called a holographic will and is permitted in life-or-death situations the law calls *in extremis.*"

"The House of Lords in England had problems with deciding who 'Mother' was," Trace continued.

"It was well-known that the farmer called his wife 'Mother'—and that his real Mother lived with the two of them on the rural property."

"So we have the same problem—looks like," said Geri. What did the House of Lords decide, by the way?"

"They decided that the farmer meant for his *wife* to have the farm and entire estate.

Which makes sense. His mother was aged and had no use for any of it. His wife had children to care for," Trace explained.

"So when the Probate Court let you know there was this problem, did you say to them that the ex-wife was likely the intended beneficiary?"

"No, I said the *daughter*—Norma.

As in the English case, and following the legal precedent that it set—the Probate Court of New Hampshire must decide what the intention of the testator was. This is *always* difficult with a holographic will that is signed by the testator *without witnesses*.

I think Miles meant for *Norma* to be left with some degree of material security. She was his only child.

I don't think he really gave much thought to his ex—who had remarried anyways."

"So does this official letter in this package confirm that?" Geri asked.

"Yes. They applied the rule from the English case and the American Statute of Wills—which applies to most cases in most states—except Louisiana, where French law and the Code Napoleon formed the basis for inheritance laws in that state."

"Gee, you really know a lot, Trace!" said Geri.

"I have to," he said. "I'm an attorney."

"You going to notify Norma?"

"I will send her an email and maybe chat on the phone. I think she'll be happy.

Then I'll call Helen. She should be happy too. As I told her, she will get a few million in her Easter Egg basket this year!"

“Then you should bill her but—if I know you at all—you will bill her for peanuts! Why don’t you ask her for a few thousand?

You did lots of work and put in lots of time on this! You drove to see Norma, you filed with the court. You wear the same clothes day in and day out—it’s time you had a new suit and a couple of shirts!”

Trace had an embarrassed look on his face.

“You’re right, Geri. I will put together an invoice for both of them. Thanks for the support.”

“What are friends for?” she smiled.

13

"The first thing is to grip the gun tightly—but pull the trigger softly," said Trace.

Trace and Geri were having a day off in the countryside so Geri could learn to shoot her new pistol.

"The best advice I've heard is to 'squeeze' the trigger," he said.

"Don't worry about aiming at anything right now, just get the feel of the discharge and recoil that follows."

Bang! Geri flinched slightly as the sound and shock were unfamiliar.

"Couple more!" The pistol slammed out two more rounds into the dirt about fifty yards in front.

"Good. Now—sight control. Put the front sight on the target and line up the rear sight so that the front sits in the vee—the notch. Once they line up, the bullet will go right where you want it.

See that tin can?" Geri did as Trace instructed and squeezed off a round that made the can jump about five feet into the air.

"I hit it!" she said with delight.

"This is not as hard as you thought, is it?" said Trace with a grin. "Practice makes perfect!"

"I could do this for hours!" said Geri.

"Tin cans and old bottles are one thing, but shooting a man is another," Trace said. "There's one more fundamental rule I need you to know."

Trace showed Geri how to put the safety on, and moved her arm so the barrel pointed at the ground.

"Never point your weapon at anything you don't intend to shoot. Always be aware that this gun can seriously wound or kill. You need to know if there's a round in the chamber, you need to aware of the direction in which the barrel is pointed."

"Can I use it for self-defence? That's kinda why I got it in the first place," she said.

"The law says you can use it only if your life is in danger and you are defending yourself against a deadly threat.

You can't use it to protect some third party—say, in a bank robbery and you shoot the robber. If he is not gonna shoot you personally, keep it in your holster."

"The Old West had a rule: 'Shoot first, ask questions afterward'," said Geri. "Does that still apply?"

"As an attorney, I would encourage the reverse behavior: tell them you have a gun, ask them to leave, and if the situation escalates—and it can do so very quickly—draw your weapon and fire."

"Can I shoot a few more tin cans before we call it a day?" Geri asked.

***

Penny greeted Trace as he came up the stairs into the second floor suite where his office was. The building was red brick exterior but the inside was old oak flooring and wainscotting and was starting to show its age. Trace got a bargain on a long-term lease and he didn't really need more space than this.

"Mrs. Thorne wants you to call. Also the District Attorney in Concord wants you to call. And last of all, Norma Thorne wants you to call. All of them insist that you call them immediately," said Penny with a sparkle in her eyes.

"Of course," said Trace, "They all want it ASAP. I'm starved and a bit tired from the morning. If they call again, tell them I have a headache."

Penny smiled. "I think I can manage that," she said. She put one of her famous blueberry muffins on a plate and grabbed Trace's mug and filled it to the brim with steaming hot coffee.

"Start with this," she said.

"Did I ever tell you that I love you, Penny?" said Trace—full of gratitude.

"Oh, I already knew," she said demurely.

Trace closed his door and dialed Helen Thorne. She picked up.

"I have a letter in my hand, Mr. Edger, from the insurance company. Do you want me to read you what it says?"

Trace didn't actually—but took a long swallow of coffee and said : "*Please do.*"

"They say my life insurance policy claim is *void*. They say they do not pay out benefits for deaths that are 'unsubstantiated'. I know what they are trying to do! They are pirates and robbers!"

Trace took out a notepad and pencil and jammed it into the sharpener—making a whirring grinding noise that seemed to amuse Trace—since he often did it during his day.

He told Helen to read on.

"They say if it is *suicide*—no payments. They say my policy is quite clear about that. Why on earth would they assume Miles' death was a suicide?"

"*Did the Death Certificate say 'suicide'?*" Trace asked.

He realized with a shock that he had not inspected it that closely before Pete exhumed and shipped the body off to the Medical Examiner in Concord for autopsy.

"I didn't read it, Mr. Edger, so I don't know but I certainly hope that whoever filled it out was competent."

Trace thought of what Covidson had told him: that the death certificate was given to him filled in when he picked up the body. Trace observed that Covidson didn't go to any bother to question its validity.

But Trace saw right away that somebody had apparently forged the ME's signature.

Covidson didn't seem to care. He had his money and if the paperwork was dodgy—that wasn't his fault.

Trace was pretty sure the death certificate didn't say 'suicide'. That kind of thing tends to stand out.

"*If I recall,*" said Trace, "*The cause of death was listed as a heart attack. That falls under the 'Accidental' category on most insurance policies.*"

"The insurance adjuster wants to know time and place of death, circumstances of death, cause of death according to a duly licensed state medical examiner. Every darn thing," Helen said.

"*You did not receive a notarized copy of the original death certificate from Sayonara—along with their bill?*"

"No," said Helen. "Was I supposed to?"

"*Technically, Sayonara should have provided one—or asked you for your life insurance details—so they could forward one to the insurance company.*"

Trace was chewing the eraser off a brand-new yellow pencil.

"*Helen, I'm afraid we have a dilemma here. What you don't know—and I'm not sure I should tell you because it is a police matter—you need to know.*

The original certificate was in the hands of Mr. Covidson at Sayonara Funeral Services. In my professional opinion there is a substantial possibility that it was a forgery."

"I don't understand, Mr. Edger. When you say 'forgery' you mean it was fake?"

"*That's what I mean,*" he said. "*Whoever filled it out did so to obscure the real facts of Miles' demise.*"

"So what you are saying is that if the insurance adjuster questions the certificate and it turns out to be inauthentic, then they will deny my claim on *that* basis."

"*That's the problem; or at least one of them.*"

"What's the other?" asked Helen.

"The other is that after a court-ordered exhumation and subsequent autopsy, it was determined that your husband was a victim of a planned and wilful homicide."

"He was murdered," said Helen.

"Does your policy or the letter you were given say what happens if the insured party is deceased as a result of a felony or criminal activity that resulted in his death?"

"Why—yes it does," Helen said.

"The letter refers to such-and-such a *clause* in such-and-such a *paragraph* which states that benefits cannot be paid unless and until the cause of death in this manner can be proven beyond a reasonable doubt and has notarized affidavits which attest to that in accordance with the law of the State of New Hampshire."

"This is going to be difficult—since the police themselves have not proven Miles was murdered. All they have is circumstantial evidence.

They don't have a killer, they don't have a motive and they don't have a conviction that would satisfy these strict requirements set out in your policy."

"So what you are saying is that the insurance company is going to continue to balk at paying anything to me at all. In short, Mr. Edger—I'm screwed!"

"I couldn't say it better myself!" Trace spoke--but there was no one on the line anymore.

"What do I say to her?" said Trace over a Diner meal to his sidekick Geri Moore.

"She is not going to starve, Trace. You are forgetting about the fact that Osiris Inc. went public and is trading at over forty dollars just months after its initial public offering.

Both she and Norma have shares that were worth nickels and dimes when Miles bought them in his deal with Delmar Robb to give control over to him. Now they are both millionaires!"

"Yeah," said Trace. "How ironic that Miles never got to see a penny of that."

"Let me ask you a question, Trace. Do you think the arson was designed to warn us—and Helen—off the murder investigation, and for no other reason?"

Trace waved at Marla Mullins—the server in Danni's Diner that knew every regular customer and their preferences. She knew that Trace and Geri drank a lot of coffee and that Geri had a thing for their danishes.

"I'm glad you brought this up, Geri. I've been thinking—in the shower, where I do some of my best thinking—that there must have been something specific that was to have been targeted in the fire.

Whoever set that fire meant for it to burn hot enough to melt metal. So if there was computer hardware and software or paper files in filing cabinets, they would not stand a chance at 3500 degrees."

"How can they make it that *hot*?" said Geri.

"Thermite. A chemical compound that only military people really have access to. Thermite burns using the oxygen in its iron oxide component and needs no air, no outside oxygen. So you cannot put it out!

Even if wet and hosed down, it till burns until the molecular oxygen has finished reacting with the aluminum powder. Temperatures can exceed 5000 degrees!"

"That's why the firefighters didn't have a hope of dousing that blaze! They gave it everything they had in the pumper trucks but it was futile from the start!" Geri said.

"One more reason to worry that we are dealing with very dangerous people here. Assassins, terrorists, paramilitary—I don't know but I *do* know this is way above Pete McCoy's pay grade!"

***

"Let me ask you something from your policeman's point of view, Pete," Trace said.

"If Helen Thorne has anything in her home that may contain valuable data related to her husband's work, is there a possibility that her home may get torched by an arsonist too?"

"That's something that I hadn't thought about, Trace. Maybe because it's too frightening!"

"I want to see if she has something her husband was working on or stashed at home that might give me another clue as to who is doing this," Trace said.

"And we say it is 'evidence' in the investigation you mean? To justify our search & seizure?"

"That's my thinking, Pete. If we find something—then it occurs to me that Delmar Robb might be able to help us determine what we're looking at, whether its code or an algorithm or data that suggests what he might have been working on when Miles was abducted and killed."

"We don't have too many other leads at this point," Pete admitted.

"I will call on her and poke around in her closets—probably take Geri; she likes Geri."

"Watch out for any skeletons in those closets!" said Pete.

***

Trace and Geri parked a ways down the street and just sat.

Both were scanning for suspicious automobiles that might be staking out Helen's residence. The threatening call of last week put both of them on edge.

Satisfied there were no stalkers in view, they made their way up her walkway and knocked.

"I took some time this morning to do a bit of a survey of places in the house—or even in the shed," Helen said to Trace, "where Miles might have kept boxes or what-have-you that may be of relevance.

Can I interest you in some coffee to start?"

Geri washed a couple of mugs and dried them with a dish-towel.

Helen was a meticulous homemaker and Trace reflected that his own abode looked like a proverbial pig-pen in comparison.

"Miles seldom worked at home," Helen said. "But he did bring things home from time to time and would work until the wee hours in the study—on his computers.

I say '*computers*' plural because he always had two running at the same time—and even a *third* on some occasions."

"Coffee's good!" said Geri smacking her lips.

"It's nice isn't it? It's a mixture of Ethiopian and Kenyan beans that they call 'City Roast'—like we all live in Boston or something. Anyways, *I* like it," Helen said.

"Go on upstairs, Mr. Edger," she continued. "First door on your left is the study. Light switch is behind the door for some silly reason. Touch anything you like."

Trace sat down in a wing chair just inside the study that seemed to beckon to him; he needed to think.

Under the desk was a computer tower that contained a sizeable hard drive. Without a password, he wouldn't get in—but he knew that Delmar Robb had ways.

Probably emails were encrypted and files shielded from unwanted intrusion. Not an attorney's forte.

He unplugged the keyboard, mouse and monitor from the tower and the tower from the surge-protector on the floor.

He noticed a red memory stick on the desk and dropped it into his pocket on the way out.

"Find something?" asked Geri as Trace lugged the metal cabinet down the stairs.

"Is it okay if I take this one, Helen? Whatever is on it, it looks like Miles' main workstation and I'm guessing there will be useful information on it—if we can get into it."

"Of course you can. I'm sorry—I don't know any of Miles' passwords or anything like that," she said.

"His work was private—even from me. In any case, I wouldn't understand the first thing about software and such. I barely passed Math in high school."

Trace and Geri left shortly after and Trace slung the metal box into his trunk and covered it with a ratty old wool blanket.

"I will give Delmar a shout and take this down to Nashua when I get a moment. If you're looking for something to do—you could go with me, keep me company," Trace said.

"Oh, like I don't have a real job!" said Geri. "Pick me up at home."

***

Trace explained who Geri was—as he was ushered into a lab off a hall. Delmar had trimmed his beard so it was a moustache and goatee now. He wore a white lab coat and looked tired.

"This is confidential, Delmar. Just between us. You didn't see anything and I didn't show you anything. Agreed?" Trace heaved the box onto a table and plugged in the cord to an outlet.

Delmar brought over a monitor, mouse and keyboard and plugged them in and turned the tower on.

He sat before the screen and tapped in some commands. The first two were refused but the third try got him to Miles' dashboard and file folders.

"What are we looking for, Mr. Edger?"

"Trace. Call me Trace."

"Good name for an investigator."

"It's actually the Spanish word for '*three*'," Trace replied. "I was the *third try* after my Mother had two previous miscarriages. I was the gift from God she had prayed for."

"You never told me that!" said Geri.

"You never asked," said Trace red-faced.

Trace moved closer to the table and peered at the screen.

"We're looking for something Miles was doing that might have been of a sensitive nature, if you know what I'm saying."

Delmar did. "Okay, so some pseudocode or notes that nobody but a handful of people would ever have seen."

"Except *you*," said Trace.

"Except me—and that was of course because we worked on intelligence projects together for a while there—and I assume he didn't just quit that after we parted ways," said Delmar.

"Do you have anybody in mind?" said Trace.

"Pentagon," said Delmar. "The Army was just developing some computer vision tools and applications like facial recognition software. They got stuck and sent a couple of techies to Osiris to see if we had a fix for them."

"And *did* you?" said Trace.

"Actually we went one *better*. We redesigned or reconfigured—however you want to say it—their software architecture so that it 'exceeded expectations' shall we say.

But that was just the start," Delmar said.

"Russian hackers were very sophisticated from fairly early on," he continued. "So the Pentagon wanted us to help track and derail their efforts. They were very good at exploiting back doors into large security facilities with very sensitive information."

Geri pulled her chair closer. She was all ears.

"That might be something that Miles continued to work at after he moved to....what's that little town?"

"Earlsdale," said Trace.

"Right. Earlsdale," said Delmar—like he was equating it with Antarctica or Mongolia.

Trace spoke now. "This is one of the few hardware devices that remain," said Trace, filling Delmar in on the recent arson event.

"Jeezus! Who is on Miles' case?" Delmar exclaimed.

"Whoever it is wasn't content to snuff him—they wanted to eliminate his work as well," said Trace.

"Ok," said Delmar. "Let's get into it."

A young woman came into the lab asking for Delmar—who spoke quietly with her for a moment and then he said: "I'm sending out a lunch order for us; I don't know about you guys but I'm famished!"

"They make really creative sub sandwiches across in the plaza," said the girl.

"Thanks," said Geri. "Don't forget the coffee!" The girl smiled and swept out of the lab.

"What I see here is a cluster of files and docs that share a common theme," Delmar said shifting on his stool. "That makes me think that this was something current for him."

"What's the theme?" said Trace.

"Espionage," said Delmar.

***

The skies were darkening and threatening rain as Trace and Geri made their way back to town along New Hampshire Hwy. 9.

"The *Russians*?" Geri was not happy with the conclusions that Delmar Robb had made.

"That means that *either* side can be trying to get Miles and his innovations under *their* control. That means that they are *in competition* for those algorithms," Geri remarked.

"Still, I don't get how Miles ends up *dead*," she said.

"Maybe *one* side wanted him not to talk to the *other* side," said Trace in a somber tone.

"They could've just kidnapped him!" said Geri hotly. "Didn't have to kill the guy!"

"Maybe they just got paranoid," said Trace.

"And they're probably worried about what Miles *knew* and *we found*—with Delmar's able assistance—what was on the C: drive—and the F: drive I found on his desk."

"You sure we can trust Delmar not to have saved or exported any of that?"

"I'm sure," Trace said. "Whoever has that information is in danger. Is a *dead man*, so to speak."

"Oh that's nice!" Geri retorted. "So that information is on the computer in your trunk in the car that we are driving that may be under Russian or CIA surveillance at this very moment. Is that right?"

"Relax, Geri. You've got your nice little Smith & Wesson buddy in your handbag, don't you?"

"I feel much better now you said that," she said snidely. "Can we dump that computer tower someplace else?"

"Think we can convince Pete to take it? What's safer than a police station?" said Trace smiling.

14

"So it all comes down to what's in this metal *box*?" said Pete staring at the 18 by 12 by 18 piece of computer hardware with flat black steel frame and sides.

"Fundamentally," said Trace.

"So what is it *in here* that makes it worth a man's life?" said Pete sitting in his favorite chair in an otherwise depressing and shabby office for a senior police officer.

"Information, Pete. A certain kind of secret information that can be a real advantage for military and intelligence operatives to get their hands on."

"And you want me to do *what* with it?" said Pete.

"Why—*guard* it, Pete! Day and night! Sit on it like a hen on a metal egg!" Trace was slapping his knee.

Pete had a sour look on his face. "I'll get Monkman to put it in lockup with an evidence label. Until we figure out what to do with it."

"Did I tell you I bought Geri a gun for her birthday?" said Trace.

"How sweet of you, counselor! Was it a *big* gun?" said Pete.

"Smith & Wesson .40Cal. 9-shot magazine. Cute as a bug's ear," said Trace.

"And you made sure she has a permit to carry, right?"

"Of course. I even gave her some lessons out in the valley on an abandoned farm. She will pick it up quickly. She already said she feels more secure packing heat in her handbag. She's not the kind to hit someone with an umbrella anyway."

"I got nothing against honest citizens carrying guns around for self-protection. I carry one *myself.*"

"Yeah, well you're the Chief of Police. It goes with the badge."

"So does insomnia, back aches, too much coffee—and a 1.8% pay raise over two years!"

"But look at the bright side, Pete. You've got a new SUV this year; who knows what else will come your way?"

***

The next phone call Helen Thorne got was from a man this time. No accent.

Soon, she was sitting in Trace Edger's office drumming her fingers on the edge of his desk. Trace was chewing on another pencil eraser.

"This guy said Miles '*got what he deserved because of what he was doing with my wife*'."

"Is this the first time this person has called?" said Trace.

"Yes. Why do I get the feeling this is my deranged neighbors?"

"It might be. We need to get somebody to look into these people," said Trace. "Just to be clear—he did not threaten your safety in any way, right?"

"How do *I* know what he's going to do?" Helen complained.

"I know a private investigator who I've worked with in the past. I can refer him to you and let him do what he's good at. If there's something with the Miserly couple—he'll find out."

"What if it's *not* them?" she said.

"Well, whoever it is, we will hunt them down and make them stop. It must fit somehow with the other puzzle pieces we are holding. Must relate to Miles—in some way or other."

"I'll wait to hear from him, then," said Helen. And she was gone out the door.

Trace stood up and stretched his arms up. "I'm going for lunch, Penny. Can I get you anything?"

Trace was enough of a gentleman and thoughtful boss to always ask, even though he knew Penny always declined since she preferred to bring her own lunch—fresh fruit or salads—maybe tuna on rye with a pickle.

***

Geri was there in their usual booth. She couldn't be sure whether Danni the owner instructed Marla the waitress to save it for their exclusive use—but somehow it was always available for the bunch of them.

"Hungry?" said Geri. Trace usually ordered his usual all day-breakfast with three scrambled eggs but today he was going through the menu with an intense expression.

"I'm having the clubhouse," he said to Marla. "Large fries."

Geri ordered the soup-of-the-day combo—with choice of Caesar or potato salad.

"Why is there always somebody in this town making life difficult for somebody *else* in this town?"

Trace sounded exasperated; Geri chalked it up to hungry male behavior.

After he had eaten, he settled down. He blew on the steaming coffee that concluded his meal.

"Now that I know I'm going to survive—I'm ready to tell you what's on my mind." he said.

Trace recounted what Helen had told him. Geri listened closely.

"So all this guy did was—be thoughtless and rude? For what purpose?"

"That's why I'm talking to you, Geri. You're like the other hemisphere of my brain."

"I think I'd prefer to be called your 'right-hand woman' or something."

"Do you think this call is a *one-off*, or is it going somewhere?" said Trace.

"Sounds to me like this person wants some payoff—maybe someone who thinks she is a rich widow and is willing to fork over some cash to get some pest out of her life," Geri said.

"You mean blackmail?"

"She's an easy target, Trace."

"I've got a PI following up and once he gives me his report, I'll have a better idea of who I'm dealing with."

"One darned thing after another; this is one of your most difficult cases yet, Trace."

"Somebody is making my life difficult and it's starting to piss me off!"

***

The e-mail was revealing: it turns out that the Ecliptic Cruise was booked by *Carly*—which was consistent with the facts Trace already had.

Helen was right: these despicable people next door were setting Miles up, although their reasons were yet to be revealed.

Amateurs make stupid mistakes—and Randy and Carly Miserly were amateurs.

Helen found a handwritten note in her mailbox that said that this cruise woman was going to the lawyer and would expose Miles Thorne as a philanderer and womanizer. It stated an e-mail address where she should respond without delay.

She told Trace—who told Geri.

"This is like some cheap ransomware scam where hackers take down a hospital network and demand money to unlock the files," said Geri.

Trace said: "The person who wrote this note hand-delivered it so they either drove to her door, or..."

Geri cut him off. "...they live next door!"

"Just match the handwriting and this will bust them. I'll get the PI to pretend to solicit for some charity—and get her to fill in some form or other—then we'll do a comparison," said Trace.

The handwriting match *was* verified—Trace brought in the heavy guns.

It was just about Happy Hour and Trace suspected the couple might be already knocking back a couple of drinks when Pete McCoy pounded on the front door.

Carly swung it open in a way that said: 'Yeah, I've had a few. So what?' She was wearing a tight tank top and cutoffs and for a moment her mouth just stood open.

"*Police*," said Pete and didn't wait to be invited in. He was followed by Geri and Trace.

"Mind if we sit down?" said Pete sitting down. "We have a few questions for you and your husband."

Husband came in smelling of barbecue smoke and bourbon and demanded to know what was going on.

"I have it on good authority that you—Carly—had booked a cruise with the husband of the lady next door—whom I'm sure you know. Helen Thorne?"

To everyone's surprise—and maybe liquor played a small part in this—husband Randy started to rant that Miles was trying to have an affair behind everyone's back and little ol' Carly was just a victim of a scheming neighbor.

Carly booked the trip because Miles pressured her, he claimed.

Then, Geri jumped to her feet and started defending Miles and Helen. She shook her fist in Randy's face and glared at Carly calling them phonies and charlatans.

Pete was really enjoying the hubbub. This was behavior he could understand! He understood people—not software, not hardware!

Trace intervened by stepping between Geri and Randy and raising his hands in the air.

"Let's all calm down here, folks," he said like he was a therapist in a group therapy session.

Pete just kept on grinning like an idiot. He would have kind of fit in with group therapy right about then.

"What are you two really up to?" said Trace—looking mostly at Carly since she was the one with cleavage.

"You don't expect us to believe that Miles Thorne was in any way, shape or form involved with Carly, now do you?" he continued.

Randy wanted to speak but he slumped into a chair.

"If you are thinking you are going to blackmail Helen Thorne by perpetrating this ridiculous tale of lust and deception," Trace said in his best lawyerly tone of voice, "...then I'm going to have Chief McCoy arrest you *right now*."

That made things a bit quieter. Even Pete took off his hat and scratched his scalp.

"Arrest us for *what*?" said Carly with that impudent tone.

"On suspicion of *murder*, " Trace bluffed. He was way out on a limb so he tried to avoid looking at Geri in case she smiled or giggled.

"We will say that you killed Miles because he was trying to steal Carly away from you," Trace said looking dead center at Randy who was gawking at everyone from his seat.

"We will tell the court that you were the jealous husband who flew into a rage," Trace continued.

"It was *you* that phoned Helen the other night, wasn't it Randy? And it was *you* who scribbled the note in her mailbox, wasn't it Carly?"

They seemed to melt into the furniture.

"Yeah—and you know *what*?" Geri shouted—still on her feet; she wasn't done.

"I will write a news clip for the *Examiner* and put the headline right on Page One: '***Murder suspect and wife blackmail local widow.***'"

Carly flung herself at Randy's feet mewing like a cat—asking him why he made her do it, blah blah blah —and Randy was stroking her hair and saying: 'It's okay, kitten, it was just a joke, okay?'

Trace took Geri by the hand and led her toward the door—and on the way plopped Pete's hat back on his head, saying: "I think we're *done* here."

***

Trace Edger was sitting in his office reading state legislation about testamentary trusts when Penny put through an urgent call.

"Mr. Edger? It's *Norma Thorne.* I hope you remember me. You *paid me a visit* at my apartment not too long ago?"

"*Of course I remember, Norma. I am just getting down to executing your Father's will—now that the Probate Court has finally finished with it.*

You sound upset; what happened?"

"You're damned right I'm upset! My apartment was burglarized and everything was turned upside down!"

"*When did this happen Norma? Have you notified the local police?"*

"Yes, the police have come and gone. They asked if any jewellery or cash was stolen and when I said 'No' they advised me to call my insurance agent!

How do you like *that*? No fingerprint collection, no shoe impression photographs, no indication of any interest on their part to lift a finger to help me!"

"*I guess this is a pretty routine case and unless you were assaulted, they don't think much of it,*" Trace said.

"My dog Muffy is so terrified she won't come out from under the bed!" Norma went on.

"*Let me ask you a question, Norma. Did you have any software or hard drives that might have had some of the data your father had collected during his time in Nashua*?

I can tell you in confidence that some of his work and some of his customers were top secret projects with certain government departments."

"No. Dad never did any work when he was at home and after he left he took everything but his old toothbrush. He never came to the apartment so there is nothing of his *here*."

"*Let me go at this from another angle*," Trace continued. "*Was the ransacking of your place what you would expect of a common burglar looking for stuff to fence for drug money?*"

"They took my computer. Is that significant?"

"*That is not characteristic of ordinary burglars, no. They want a certain kind of information or data that may be stored on your computer. Do you have backup files?*"

"You think this is related to my Father's work? Am I in danger, Mr. Edger?"

"*I wish I could answer that, Norma. My investigation here in Earlsdale is taking some weird twists and turns. But if someone knows you are Miles Thorne's daughter, we might have a problem.*

Listen—would you be able to relocate in Earlsdale for a short while—until our investigation is concluded?"

"So you mean *I am* in danger! They may kidnap me or torture me or something, is that it?"

"*At this point in time, I have no idea what their next move is going to be, but I would be more comfortable if you were close by where the local police and I could keep you on our radar,*" Trace said.

"Can you find me a hotel? That permits dogs?"

***

Pete called Trace and met him for breakfast at the Diner.

"Got a local disturbance call last night," Pete started as he ordered his usual.

""What kind of disturbance?" said Trace.

"House party. Music, cars racing in the street outside. Kids out on Twilight Road."

Pete looked at Trace; Trace looked at Pete.

"You're not gonna say anything?" Pete inquired. "Isn't that where Mr. Mortician picked up Miles Thorne's body from?"

"You saying this is the *same* address?" said Trace.

"Russians," Pete said. "The place is owned by a Russian gangster who is known to State Police and the FBI."

"Jeez, that's a bit scary. Why would they have a place in our little nowhere town?" said Trace.

"Exactly. Why here? What is their interest in Earlsdale? Not a big market for drugs or any other criminal enterprise."

"Maybe they are hiding out here. In deep cover."

"Can't be too deep if the Feds know they are here," said Pete.

"Good point. You think they were responsible for the burning of Miles' office and adjacent warehouse?"

"I can't think of why *locals*—like delinquent kids—would pull a stunt like that. We agree this was a pro job— what with the thermite and all."

"So did you bust up the party?"

"I tried to. McFee and Monkman handed out tickets to the fast 'n furious types on the road for speeding, DUI and no registration tags.

I went inside and the music got turned down and I told them the noise level was bothering the neighbors and I would issue a ticket for public nuisance if this continued."

"And they just meekly complied because you are the Chief of Police, right?"

"No. A rather large Russian-speaking guy came out of the back room and said '*Vsyoh*' and nodded to some of the boys—and that's what did the trick. I didn't recognize the guy but he looked like someone I wouldn't want to mess with."

"Why didn't we check this place out—after we made Covidson tell us where he picked up the body?""He initially *lied*, Trace. He gave us the wrong address, or at least *not* the *real* address where the body was left out in the lawn chair. We discovered that *later*.

"Good thing the neighbors didn't see *that*," said Trace. "*That* would have created a disturbance."

***

"Hello again, Norma," said Geri cheerily. "What brings you to Earlsdale?"

They were in the Diner on their lunch and Trace was treating.

"Mr. Edger thought I should come to town to...umm...do some sightseeing, get out of the big city."

Geri gave a querying look to Trace.

"Well, the fact is somebody tossed her apartment and I think she may be in danger if she stays there," said Trace stirring his coffee.

"My God, Norma! Did they do a lot of damage? Did they *threaten* you?" Geri reached instinctively for Norma's hand.

"No, well, I wasn't there—but Muffy was *traumatized.*"

"Where are you staying here?" said Geri.

"At the Regent Hotel. That's where the dog is right now," said Norma.

"You come and stay with me in my condo," said Geri firmly. "I'm happy to have you and Muffy!"

Norma blushed and put her face in her cup. "I don't want to be a bother to anyone..."

"Nonsense! You will keep me company and I will get to show you the handful of stores worth browsing at in town."

Trace smiled and thanked Geri.

"The other good news, of course, is that Norma gets to see what her father left to her in the will," said Trace. "I think this is going to please you, Norma. I know you probably didn't expect it."

"When you called me to say that I was named in the will I couldn't believe it!" she said. "Is it a complicated process—what you do—Mr. Edger?"

Geri looked at Trace wondering if he would mention the court's conflict with Norma's mother's lawyer about who was the *intended* beneficiary of the money.

"Did your father ever call you 'Precious Princess'?" Trace asked.

"Yes! That is what he called me when I was little. I loved being his little princess!"

"But he never would have called your birth mother by that name, right?"

"Are you *kidding*? '*Bat Outta Hell*' he would have called her—if he had had a nickname for her."

Geri giggled. "Sorry. It's just a bit funny."

Norma smiled and you could see relief written all over her face.

She had a new friend in Geri. And of course, the rugged Hero archetype in Trace Edger. Geri wondered if the little girl inside of Norma Thorne would now be able to stand up and live the life she surely deserved.

***

"Hey, Trace. Wanna come down to the station—if you got time?" Pete was on the phone.

Trace always had time for Pete McCoy. They were professionals in two closely-related fields, but over time had become much more like friends.

"What's up, Chief?" said Trace sauntering in to the station. Trace remembered the cappuccinos. He remembered his friend was addicted to Beanbags cappuccinos.

"My old Dodge? The *Charger*? With 300,000 miles on it? Out back in the lot?"

"Yeah," said Trace. "Did it start up and drive away on you?" He was smiling but soon stopped.

"Somebody set it on fire last night! It's completely burnt out!" said Pete.

"You're kidding me, right?"

"Must have happened in the wee hours but nobody reported it. The fire department didn't get a call and didn't know anything about it until I called them after I got to work."

"This is payback for the Russian party visit," said Trace.

"You think? How do I respond to this?"

"They want to get a rise out of you, Pete. They threaten people. They want you to understand you are messing with the wrong people."

"I probably *am*," said Pete. "So what do you recommend, counselor?" Pete slurped the foam off his coffee.

"They maybe think you are a small-town cop who will go and question them about it, and act all self-righteous. But you won't do that. You will just add it to our file of clues.

Every thing these people do leads us one step closer to finding out who is pulling the strings. And who decided Miles Thorne had to die.

Because—Pete! They are going to make a *mistake*. And when they do—we are going to be right there—with a set of handcuffs!"

***

Dave McComb—Pete's deputy—drifted in and hung up his coat. He greeted Trace.

"The quality of automobiles in this town is getting better and better," McComb said.

"I just handed out a three-hundred dollar fine to some dude in a red Porsche Targa 911 out on Highway 9."

McComb put on the kettle to make a coffee and stuck his spoon in the jar of instant dark roast and dumped that in his mug.

"Doing close to one-forty when he blew past me. I got to put the pedal to the metal on our new SUV finally!" McComb said with obvious excitement.

Now Trace shifted in his chair and grinned. "So does the SUV do one-forty *too*?" he said to McComb.

Pete intervened. "Hey! This new police car has a 427 Hemi—with fuel-injection and overhead cams!" Pete was proud of his new police car.

"I flashed him and he pulled over," said McComb taking his seat. He blew on his coffee.

"Funny thing is—there were two of them in the car. Fancy-dressed older guy with muscles and a gold chain that would choke a bulldog.

And a nice blonde babe a bit younger. Hard to see her eye color with the sunglasses but they kinda *reeked* money," said McComb.

"So...not tourists?" Pete said.

"Not tourists. But they were speaking Russian to each other," McComb said.

"Russian? You speak Russian, Dave?" said Pete with astonishment.

"*Nyet*," said Dave. "But I grew up in a Russian neighborhood in Boston so I know the sound of the language."

"Well, what were they saying?" asked Pete.

"I don't speak it *that* well, Chief," McComb admitted.

Pete looked at Trace. "Well?"

"Well, there seems to be a new neighborhood forming right here in Earlsdale," said Trace. "I don't mind but I wonder whether there's something going on that we should be aware of."

"Meantime, I'll just hang out on Highway 9 and write speeding tickets," said McComb. "The Mayor should be happy that we're contributing to the city coffers and paying her salary."

***

"How did you get into journalism?" Norma was asking Geri.

They were enjoying the sunset colors over Lake Wendigo from Geri's condo balcony. Geri had finally an excuse to open a bottle of gin since she was not one to drink alone.

"I was curious; 'nosy' my family used to say. I always wanted to know the story behind the story. I wanted to know why people did what they *did* that got them in trouble."

"Why not a career in psychology, then?" said Norma.

"Too cerebral, too intellectual. I like to get my feet muddy and wade into it," Geri said.

"So where did you get your first job—as a journalist I mean?" Norma jiggled the ice in her gin and tonic.

"In Boston. My Dad was a Congressman at that time and he knew people in the newspaper world. In those days it was still driven by print media and television was not the preferred way of presenting the news."

"You must be older than you look!" Norma blurted out—then apologized.

"Hehe, well, I was already in the business when Steve Jobs invented his first Apple computer. It wasn't even a MacIntosh at that point."

Muffy started barking at somebody down on the sidewalk. Geri put her drink down and peered over the railing.

"Just someone with a bigger dog," she said at length.

Norma had seen Geri's sweater ride up enough to show a holster on her hip.

"You carry a gun?" Norma said with eyes wide.

"You know, I'm getting used to it. I forget it's there." Geri said. "But yes—lately I've been thinking more carefully about what is around me."

"Ever been married?" Norma asked.

"I was—for a while," Geri said. "Hot shot salesman who swept me off my feet with his sales pitch, I guess." Geri refilled their glasses with a bit more gin this time.

"What happened? Any kids?"

"No kids, Norma. Perhaps it was for the best.

I would never have had the career I have if I had chosen motherhood.

Besides, my ex would never have been around much to see his kids grow up. He had big dreams and in time—I realized they were bigger than *we were as a couple.*"

"I'm sorry," Norma said. "My parents were divorced too."

"Yes, I know, Norma. And I feel badly for you. I know you suffered."

Geri topped up the glasses with tonic water. "But life goes on, sweetie."

"Yes, I guess so," Norma said.

"No prospects for your love-life?" teased Geri.

"Other than the deadbeat—I haven't had much experience with men," Norma said.

"We'll see what we can do about *that*!" said Geri. "You're in *my* town, now!"

15

Trace had just settled in at his desk after greeting Penny and getting handed a juicy fresh blueberry muffin to go with his morning java.

Pete hadn't stayed put in his own office, however. He stomped up the stairs and greeted Penny—who waved him into the inner part of the law office.

"We've got a problem!" said Pete out of breath. Penny brought him a coffee in a styrofoam cup and Pete gratefully took it.

"Helen Thorne called this morning. She was out of town for a couple of days apparently. Got an elderly mother we didn't know about in a nursing home in Concord."

Pete downed the coffee and asked for a refill. Trace knew Pete was agitated about something.

"When she got home, the back door was jimmied and open. Nothing downstairs had been touched. But up in the room that was Miles' study it was an ungodly mess! Every drawer pulled out, desk turned over.

She freaked out of course and called me immediately."

"That's *two* in two weeks," said Trace soberly.

"Two *what*?" said Pete.

"Two break-ins to the residence of two people closely connected to Miles Thorne," said Trace.

He filled Pete in on Norma's break & enter story.

"They must be getting desperate," Pete said. "What on gawd's-green-earth are they looking for?"

"Probably what's on that computer I gave you and you have locked up somewhere in the police station," Trace said.

"Right! That came from Helen's, didn't it? But they couldn't find it, so they tore the place apart looking for it," said Pete.

"I'll tell you what worries me, Pete. If they can't get the hardware they want, will they go after the people who knew Miles—thinking they must have information about where Miles' secret documents are hidden!"

"You really think that would *happen*?"Pete said.

"It's just a thought—but one that won't go away," Trace said.

***

Geri was having coffee with Trace and Norma at *her* place—for a change.

Norma had settled in—and the two of them were thick as thieves!

"Doesn't she make the *best* coffee?" Norma enthused as they sat around the dining room table.

Muffy—her small dog—was asleep by Norma's feet and snoring softly.

"She *does*, Norma. She knows coffee like I know...my law books!" he grinned.

"Trace and I confer constantly on what needs to be discussed for the cases we're working on," Geri explained.

"Oh! I should leave you two in private!" said Norma.

"Not necessary," said Trace. "What I have to tell Geri concerns *you* too," he said.

"Helen Thorne's home up on the hill was raided while she was away. They did the same thing to *her* place as they did to *yours*, Norma."

"My stepmom's place? They broke in and took her computer stuff?"

Trace said that he had removed the main tower some time before and it was stored in a very safe location.

"Who is *doing* this?" said Norma, visibly upset.

"But no *phone calls*?" said Geri.

"Not this time—but then Helen was out of town for a couple of days and they may have called—but she did not report that to Pete," said Trace.

"Who is *Pete*?" said Norma.

"Chief of Police. He works closely with Geri and me—who help him on local criminal cases."

"This is bigger than I t*hought*!" mumbled Norma. "Now I see why Geri carries a weapon."

"*He* taught me how to shoot it!" Geri said enthusiastically pointing at Trace.

"You guys aren't up against The Girl Guides here, are you? Guns, burglary, arson." Norma frowned.

"Don't forget murder," said Trace. "These men are the ones who murdered your father, we believe."

Norma's reply was quick and savage.

"Get me a goddamned gun, then—I'll shoot them myself!"

16

Thumbs Elliott was the proprietor of the popular Green Thumb Garden Center out on Highway 9 west of NH Highway 123 in the far southwest corner of town.

She had built her business patiently over time using the insurance money from her husband's untimely death—and then from the thriving profits of a retail garden center that drew people from as faraway as Keene to the west and Concord and Hillborough to the east, and sometimes from Boston two hour south.

She had hired a crack team of horticultural experts—from university majors in botany to farmers looking to make a little money when the growing season wasn't growing anything.

She sold evergreen and deciduous tree saplings, perennial climbing shrubs, bulbs for any flower that could be be planted in the fall.

She sold roto-tillers and shovels and wheelbarrows. There was a mountain of peat moss and topsoil sold by the cubic foot.

There were racks of seeds for vegetables, flowers and herbs and always some helpful young employee standing by to provide advice and assistance. The *New Hampshire Gardener* magazine called Green Thumb '...the best little garden shop in New England.'

It was, of course, primarily of interest to home gardeners and local landscapers.

It only became of interest to Trace Edger and Pete McCoy because it happened to be across from the cemetery. The same cemetery that was owned and operated by Ken Covidson of *Sayonara Funeral Services*.

The same cemetery that mysteriously, accidentally buried Miles Thorne—who should not have been buried because he should not have been dead!

So Pete was just trying to decide whether to stay in his office and drink instant coffee with McComb—or go to Beanbags on Main to get a real coffee. His phone rang.

It was Thumbs Elliott. She said: "I think you should know something, Chief McCoy. There's some funny business going on at night in the cemetery. Can we meet for coffee?"

That settled it. Beanbags in half an hour!

Pete called Trace Edger who was in his office having similar thoughts about *his* morning coffee.

Chief McCoy was royalty as far as the local Beanbags people were concerned. He got served ahead of everyone, he got a table when there wasn't one. He never was allowed to pay a nickel for anything he was served.

So King McCoy was sitting by the window when Thumbs drifted it and sat down. She was soon followed by Trace—and they ordered some pastries to go with the coffees.

"So what's gotten our favorite gardener in a lather today?" said Pete.

"It's the *cemetery*. After twenty years of staring at its iron fence and its rows of headstones I notice any little change.

They are digging by *night*—and I've *never* seen that before!"

Thumbs was in her forties, in good shape, and tied her long hair that was now a mix of blonde and grey into a braid and pinned it up. Her eyes were round now with emotion and she peered into Trace's as if looking for something she couldn't find.

"That's a little strange," Trace admitted. "They have all day everyday to dig graves. Doesn't make sense."

"Are they planning to have a big influx of dead people or something?" Thumbs wondered.

"I sincerely hope not," said Trace. "It's private property, Thumbs, so I can't just go in there and say 'stop' or even 'what are you doing?'"

"But am I making *sense* here, fellas? Something just isn't right and although I'm no expert on the law, I know that someone is using the cover of night to do something they might want to conceal."

She bit into a danish—and caught the apple slice that tried to slide out of her mouth and down her chin.

"Well, I could take a drive out there later with McComb," said Pete, "if it makes you happy."

Trace warned: "We must do *nothing* that will alarm them. I don't have a problem driving you out in *my* car *out of* uniform: we'll train my binoculars on them. What time do you close in the evening, Thumbs?"

"These days, about nine. Half hour before dark.

But," she added, "...they don't seem to follow a clock; they just wait until it's very quiet and very dark, and then start moving earth and concrete slabs.

I'm sure it's all got a logical explanation. I'm just being a nosy neighbor," she concluded.

"We'll be there before closing tonight," said Trace. "I want to see this for myself."

***

The hour was getting late. Thumbs had tried to make the men comfortable but they had preferred to sit in Trace's silver Beemer with tinted windows—sipping hot chocolate.

"We don't really know what we're looking for, Pete" said Trace Edger.

"How do you mean that?" replied Pete.

"I mean, we have no idea how many bodies they bury per week or what kind of grave their clients want," Trace said. "Some want a simple casket lowered into the earth—others want a bombproof concrete bunker with a sealed steel casket for their dearly belated beloved."

"So what you're saying is that whatever commotion they are making, it's more or less normal for a mortuary in a town of this size."

"Couldn't say it better myself, Pete."

"But we haven't answered the question: *why at night*?"

"Well if they are at it tonight, maybe we'll stroll over and ask them," Trace said.

As if in response, bright lighting was switched on and a front-end loader engine fired up.

Shadows passed in front of the glare as several men were congregating maybe fifty yards into the burial ground just off a service road. There was a pickup truck from which men were offloading steel rods and sacks which looked heavy enough to be sand or maybe sawdust.

"Shall we?" offered Trace.

"Yup." said Pete, struggling into his coat. "What if the boss isn't there?" he asked.

"If nobody recognizes us, we'll say we ran out of gas on the highway—and ask where the nearest gas station is," said Trace.

"Hmmm, could work," said Pete. "What if they *do* recognize us?"

"Then we'll ask for their permit to be grave-digging by night."

"Do they need a permit for that?"

"How the hell do I know? I'm pretty sure they don't. So you yell at them—and say you'll let them off with a warning this time, and we casually walk outta there!"

"Dang. I see why you're the lawyer and I'm not."

The wide wrought iron gates were fully open and the two men advanced toward the lights.

Trace briefly checked that the safety was on—as his hand instinctively moved to his right hip where the gun was holstered.

They paused under the trees. A big man with huge shoulders and chest was gesturing with Ken Covidson near the edge of a freshly-dug hole. The soil was piled beside it and men were down inside with shovels slugging out the last of the dirt.

"That's the guy I saw at the party," Pete whispered. "Built like a Russian tank."

"He seems to be giving direction to the boss—look at how we waves his arms," Trace said quietly.

"What do we do now?" Pete inquired.

"We back off and see if we can collar Covidson on his way back to his place of business."

They retreated across the road to the garden center parking lot and waited in the car. Just a dozen yards west of the garden center was the funeral home and mortuary that managed the cemetery.

It was now half-past midnight. Somewhere an owl hooted. A sliver of moon hung in the sky.

Quite abruptly, a black Mercedes rocketed out of the gates and swung right and drove east on the highway. Nobody noticed the grey car with two men in it.

Shortly after, a short man also exited the grounds and crossed the highway to the mortuary complex.

Trace cranked the motor and gunned it.

They caught the fellow in the high beams as a cloud of dust surrounded them.

"Mr. Covidson? May we have a *word*?" Pete had his police voice on. It had a combination of authority and casualness to it. Trace called it 'soothing menace'.

"Who *are* you? What do you *want*?" Covidson was clearly taken aback.

Pete flashed his badge. "You wanna talk out here? Or inside?"

Covidson led them through the front gateway to a side door into the building.

He seemed to avoid his office for some reason—and led them to the Comfort Room where plush settees and potted palms and soft lighting was installed for grieving family waiting for a final viewing.

"A bit *late* to be out, isn't it?" Pete continued with that voice. *Soothing menace.*

"I work at hours that suit my clients," he protested. "They pay for it."

"I'm sure they do," said Pete. "Busy lately are we?"

"I don't quite understand why the police are here ," the small man bleated.

Now Pete pulled an ace that had just been given him.

"Do you have a *permit* for grave-digging at night?" he said triumphantly.

"I...I wasn't aware I needed one," said Covidson.

Trace stepped in now—he wasn't going to let Pete have all the fun!

"'*Municipal Regulation 2020-7-N*: no construction or noise or disturbance shall take place between the hours of 8:00pm and 8:00am within the municipality unless an express permit and city council approval have been applied for and obtained.'"

Pete could only marvel at the stream of legalese that issued from Trace Edger's lips—and after midnight, too!

Trace knew full well there was no such regulation but it suddenly put the fear of God in the funeral director. He turned white as a coffin shroud and wrung his hands.

"Geez, I musta missed that one, fellas," he said, now playing the sycophant and being all buddy-buddy.

"Can I pay the fine right now and be done with this unpleasant business?" said Covidson.

Pete surprised him with his response.

"We can waive the fine if you tell me what I want to know. (Pause)

I want to know who *that man was* who was at the grave site. Name, address, phone number, shoe size—whatever you got on him," said Pete.

Covidson stayed pale and said: "He wishes to remain private. To put it bluntly, if I tell you anything he will put *me* in that hole and *fill it in!*"

Pete and Trace looked at each other. Pete scratched his stubble and thought about what to say next.

"Okay—let's do it this way. You don't have to *say* a word; you just nod if what I say is correct—and shake your head if it is *not* correct.

Get me?" Covidson nodded.

"Good. First question: is this guy Russian?"

Nod.

"Is he paying you to arrange burials in advance? Like prepaid parking for dead bodies?"

Another clear nod.

"Is this an arrangement you normally have with...customers?"

The funeral director shook his head, and looked down.

"Did this guy give an address out on Twilight Road? The exact same place you picked up Miles Thornes' lifeless body?

Quick nod.

Covidson got up and pulled back the curtain briefly so he could see the street and front of the building, then let it fall closed again.

"Do you have any reason at all to believe that this guy and his team may have been responsible for the death of Miles Thorne?"

Covidson swallowed, then nodded slowly.

"Last question—does he pay you in cash?"

The director gave a little nod.

"There! That wasn't so hard, was it?" Pete said. Soothing menace again.

Pete and Trace got to their feet and let themselves out.

Trace drove back to town slowly. He was thinking.

"I have to say, Pete, I don't feel good about this.

Whatever is about to happen is something where we will have to do more than stand by and witness. We are going to have to *stop* it!"

17

Geri, Trace and Chief McCoy were having the All-Day Breakfast at Danni's Diner. It was close to six o'clock on a Thursday evening. They were deep in conversation.

"This is like Russian-Roulette," said Geri. "Someone is going to die—but we don't know *who*!"

"And the Russians aren't giving us that information," said Pete. "And Mr. Disease the Funeral Director probably is in the dark as well. They stuffed his wallet with cash—so *he's* happy."

"Let's be logical," said the attorney. "The cluster of victims has been Miles and his immediate family. Notice that Delmar Robb was not targeted. Only Norma and Helen."

"What about my old Dodge?" complained Pete.

"Awww, you would've paid someone to get rid of it, Pete—just taking up space in your lot!"

Trace was trying to inject a bit of humor into an otherwise grim situation.

"They may or may not know that Miles' home computer is ensconced safely in your police station, Pete.

In any event, it is unlikely they will try and bust in and get it," Trace continued.

"So what is the next best thing to having the computer itself?" said Pete.

"Somebody who *knows Miles* well enough to know his habits and have access to his files," said Trace.

"Helen!" Geri almost shouted.

"So maybe we should take a drive up to Opal Crescent to see if she has received any more phone calls or other things that smell like 'harassment,'" said Pete.

"Let's do that," Trace and Geri agreed.

The July day was cool as the sun went down and a wind off the lake could be felt pretty much all over town. Dark rain clouds were threatening a shower or two and most tourists and visitors were already hiding out in the cafes and restaurants. The slanting sun had now disappeared behind the hills west of town.

Pete pulled up at the address. He knocked loudly. No response. He knocked again. Nada.

Pete led them around back through a gate to the back door. Last time he was here, it had been jimmied open. This time it was just hanging open and they stepped inside.

"Helen?" Geri called out. "Helen, are you *here*?"

Geri saw Helen's purse on the kitchen table—and her cell phone and keys beside it. To her, this suggested she was just coming home and just about to go out.

But no sign of the woman herself.

Geri turned in alarm to Pete and Trace. "You don't think...?"

Trace and Pete snapped on the outside light and pulled Geri with them—slamming the back door hard enough so they could hear the lock click.

Pete got on the police radio to his men: McComb, Monkman and McFee. The entire police force of Earlsdale was about to descend on the town cemetery out on Highway 9.

Pete and Trace were upset and were arguing whether they should just charge into the cemetery grounds— or stop and grill Ken Covidson at the funeral home—which might end up being a waste of time.

Geri's intuition was usually correct—and her gut feeling was that time was of the utmost urgency if they had taken Helen Thorne.

Geri kept thinking of a yawning grave and she urged Pete to hurry.

Pete deferred to Trace. The GMC flew into the parking space in front —and Trace fairly broke down the front door.

Sharon the secretary asked if she could help him—but Trace blew past her into Covidson's office.

The man was sitting at his desk but Trace lifted him by his collar to his feet in one motion.

"Where is Helen Thorne?" he said menacingly.

"Who?" Covidson tried to wriggle out of the grip.

"Tell me—or I break your neck right here!"

"Over there," he said weakly. "The last one on the right."

Trace realized he meant the cemetery.

He pushed the man back into his chair hard enough to topple him backwards.

"You fuck!" he spat as he rushed to the front door.

"They've got her!" said Trace breathlessly and Pete gunned it across three lanes of blacktop and a gravel shoulder and through the gates.

A man Trace had never seen was standing at graveside with a svelte blonde woman wearing black.

A casual visitor might have mistaken them for mourners.

The two only looked up because the SUV skidded to a stop—and close behind it another police car—which emptied out quickly.

Monkman and McFee stepped into the light and pointed shotguns at the man, motioning for him to lay down flat with his hands behind his head.

The blonde made a run for it. She didn't get far. Geri drew her pistol and placed two quick shots into her body and she screamed and collapsed on the sod.

"The casket!" shouted Geri. "Get the casket out!"

McComb and Pete got a rope from the trunk and together with Trace, wedged it under the wooden box that lay in the hole and hauled for all they were worth. The box now sat upright on the damp grass.

A woman's voice from inside called for help; Pete grabbed a shovel laying nearby and jammed it under the edge of the lid. He put his full weight on it as he pried along the narrow edge until the squeal of nails told him he was in.

"Helen! Oh my God! Are you alright?" Geri lifted the woman under the arms so that she could sit up and catch her breath.

"They wanted to...I couldn't..."

"Don't try to talk, Helen. It's going to be alright now. We've got you!" Geri slipped out of her jacket and draped it around Helen Thorne's icy shoulders.

At length, Geri helped her step out of her deadly coffin and walked her over to the SUV.

Trace looked at Monkman and McFee. "I never knew you guys had *real* guns!" he said.

McFee grinned wolfishly. "Never *needed* 'em!" he said.

"What's your name?" said Trace as the man in cuffs was hustled back to the older cruiser.

"Gunter. Gunter Gross."

The East German, thought Trace. *No wonder he can speak Russian.*

Pete and Monkman lifted the bloodied Martina Karova to her feet and led her back to the rear car—at which point Monkman slipped zipties around her wrists and ankles before lifting her into the back seat of the car.

Pete did his cop thing and read them their rights, before slamming the back door of the old Dodge and came up and leaped into the driver's seat of the big Chevy. Geri was in back with Helen.

McFee secured Gross and Karova in the back seat of the other cruiser with more zipties on each one—'just to be sure' he said.

Trace noticed as the vehicles reached the highway and sped into town that the windows at Sayonara Funeral Services were all dark now.

18

"I called the FBI and they are on the way," said Pete. "They seemed quite impressed that we collared this German thug. They've been watching him but he's a sly one."

"My concern is that we build a case to nail him not only for kidnapping and attempted murder of Helen Thorne—but also of her husband!

Only someone really dirty and desperate would do this to the Thorne family. And this Gunter fellow fits the profile—he is the missing link that can let us connect the dots."

"He sold out to the Russians, you mean?" said Geri.

"He sold secret information that the CIA was paying for, and he sold it to America's enemy," said Trace.

"If there's one thing I *really* hate it's a traitor!" he said.

"Don't you need a confession?" said Geri.

"Circumstantial evidence will prove he is behind all of it," said Trace. "If this were East Germany in 1975 he would be tortured; I'm not big on torture but he deserves the full weight of the law!

I'm going to work closely with Pete, and the DA and the FBI to ensure this guy never eats another ice cream cone as long as he lives!"

"Can we impound his car?" said Pete hopefully. "I've never had a Porsche police car—although the Saudis or Kuwaitis apparently have them."

"Until the prosecutors decide what will happen here, so far as I am concerned—this red car is a material asset used to facilitate a felony and can be impounded *indefinitely,*" Trace declared.

He added: "If you want to drive it around, Pete—I'll be the last one to say anything!"

"Will Martina be okay?" Geri said timidly. "I got a little carried away there when I saw what they had done to Helen."

"She is recovering in Concord General and is under supervision by local law enforcement. They put a tracking collar on her ankle in case she goes to the bathroom and forgets to come back!" said Pete.

"Norma and I are going to get some groceries and a bouquet of roses and head up to Helen's house for dinner. I told her we are doing the cooking—and she is to relax and open a bottle of wine," said Geri.

"I'll be honest with you," said Trace. "When I realized she was in a coffin down in that hole, my heart was pounding something awful! I felt that it would be my fault if they murdered her too—and I really didn't want to live with that!"

"Can I say something *else*?" said Trace.

"Those were two *amazing* shots you put in that girl, Geri—and strange as it may sound—I'm damned proud of you!"

Trace embraced Geri and squeezed hard enough to make Geri gasp for breath.

“A year ago if you told me I would own a gun and use it to shoot a criminal—I would’ve told you you were crazy!

But now when I look at it—I wonder why I didn’t take steps to protect myself years ago?” she said. “Are they going to lay charges against me for shooting her?”

“Geri—you were acting at the time as an *ad hoc* law enforcement officer,” said Pete. “So—no!”

“Where did you pick up that little Latin phrase, Pete? You never cease to astonish me!” said Trace.

“You’d be amazed at what I know,” said Pete. “I’m the Chief of Police!”

“You sure are, Pete!” said Geri hugging him as well.

19

Lunch today was at a new steak house that had opened up on Peter Street—conveniently close to City Hall and the Council Chambers. Like many new restaurants during their honeymoon phase, it was chock-full.

But since Mayor Margot Han herself made the reservations, there was a lovely table set aside for her party.

"I want to hear about it from beginning to end, Trace," the Mayor said. "Like a bedtime story!"

With Trace Edger was Chief McCoy, Geri Moore and Norma Thorne. Helen Thorne had been invited but had caught cold after her misadventure in the graveyard so was staying home to nurse it.

So Trace gave Mayor Han the highlights of their adventures in ten minutes flat.

Then the group turned their attention to the champagne that was being served.

The menu offered steak in various styles such as T-Bone, Texas-style, tenderloin—cooked to one's preference.

The sides were good old standards like New Hampshire organic red potatoes, green salads with organic, non-GMO local vegetables, fresh asparagus, and locally baked fruit pies for dessert.

The in-house barista did wonders with coffee so everyone got to sample his handiwork after dinner.

"So, Norma, are you going to *stay* with us in Earlsdale? Don't go back to that big city! Crowded, stinky, full of crime!" The Mayor was being ironic. Mayor Han was a Ph.D. in Data Science so she had a sharp mind yet—to everyone's delight—a cutting wit as well.

"I'm going to try being Geri's room-mate—since she's invited me. We are having the *best* time together!"

"What plans for the summer have you guys made?" said the Mayor.

Norma responded instantly.

"Geri's going to teach me how to *shoot*!" she exclaimed.

The Mayor came right back: "I've *heard* that she put her pistol to good use the other night in the cemetery! I *love* it!"

After dinner, Mayor Han asked Trace a few questions about how the sequel to the adventure would go. He explained that the state and federal authorities were taking over the case.

"But I'll keep an eye on the funeral director in case he tries digging more graves by moonlight!" he concluded with a smile. "That is, if he avoids jail and pays the hefty fines he faces!"

"Don't you like living in a small town, Pete?" Mayor Han asked the Chief of Police.

"Nothing ever happens, right?"

Pete shook his head with disbelief and spooned out some of the froth from his coffee and noisily slurped it down.

Mayor Han turned to Geri and said: “Chief McCoy gets the arrest, you get the story—*what* does our favorite attorney get?”

Geri grinned and rubbed Trace’s shoulder affectionately. “He gets the glory!” she said.

THE END

www.ingramcontent.com/pod-product-compliance
Ingram Content Group UK Ltd.
Pitfield, Milton Keynes, MK11 3LW, UK
UKHW020415250726
13967UKWH00007B/2653

9 781989 386132